TRISTEN ROWEN

Love Never Forgets

Devenscrest Press

First published by Devenscrest Press 2021

First edition

ISBN: 978-1-7371896-0-2

This book was professionally typeset on Reedsy.
Find out more at reedsy.com

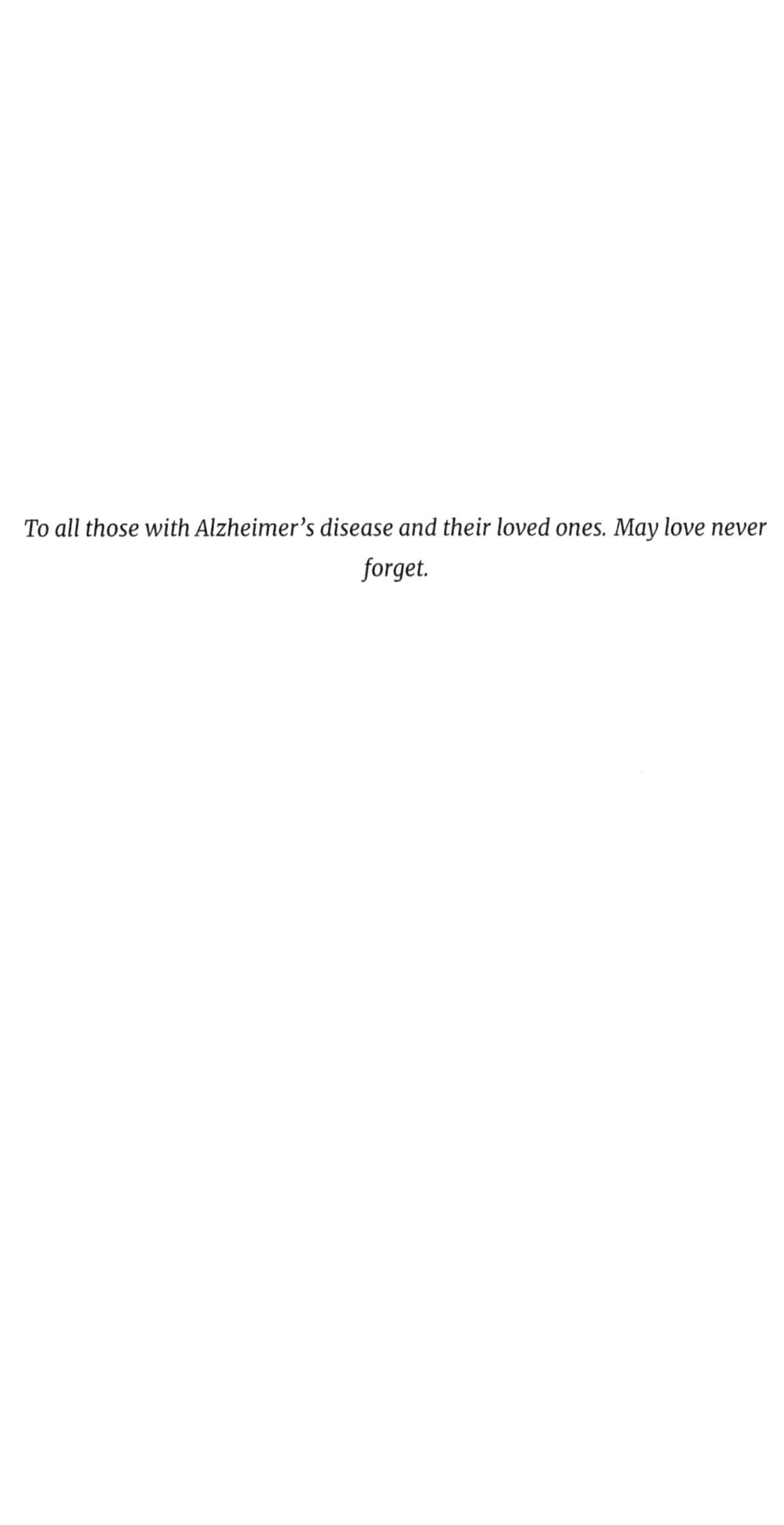

To all those with Alzheimer's disease and their loved ones. May love never forget.

Acknowledgement

I'd like to thank all my readers and followers, particularly my awesome beta readers who volunteered their time and offered invaluable insight and feedback in the final production of this story.

I'd further like to acknowledge all those individuals, spouses, and families who inspired me in the creation of this story. Their stories have not been forgotten.

1

Chapter 1

1980

On the eve of my eighteenth birthday, I sulked in the backseat of my old man's station wagon, my bratty kid brother next to me as we made the long trek up to some lake in Northern Vermont. Martha's Vineyard, Nantucket, or the Hamptons would have been better than driving out to the boonies to meet up with a childhood friend of my old man's, a guy I never met. Over the years, I must have heard countless stories of the "good ole days."

Rain pounded the windows as I stared longingly out them, dreading the unknown of what this summer might bring.

"Oh, cheer up, sweetheart," my mother said. She took out her compact mirror, making sure her bright red lipstick was done just right, not a single smudge. In a yellow sundress and matching sandals, her shoulder-length auburn hair in perfect curls, she dressed as if she were going to one of her luncheons or dinner parties. "It won't be so bad," she droned on. "Anyway, your father and Frankie haven't seen each other in years."

"Why do we have to come?" I asked. "Why couldn't Dad just go and we go to Martha's Vineyard like we always do?"

"This is a family vacation," my dad said. "I told you—"

"Yeah yeah, you both have the same birthday," I interrupted him before he told another boring childhood tale of Tommy Prescott and Frankie Lachance. We'd only been on the road for an hour with three hours to go, and he was already going on and on about this thing and that thing. I could have cared less. "And you promised each other you'd meet up again on your thirtieth, fortieth, and fiftieth birthdays. Blah, blah, blah."

"Yeah, well, I missed the last two." Again, something I already knew. "I couldn't miss this one. The big five-zero."

As a workaholic and senior partner for an advertising firm in Boston, he'd work anywhere from forty to eighty hours a week, working so much my mother worried he'd drop dead of a heart attack. This summer he forced himself to take an entire month off for a rare vacation. After a month, he planned on returning to Boston, leaving my brother, mother, and I out in the middle of nowhere until the end of August.

"Isn't this exciting?" my mother said in that fake, chipper voice of hers. "We get to spend the whole summer in a new place, meet new people, experience new things."

"Dad says we'll get to go water skiing," my twelve-year-old brother, Mike, said. "And canoeing and fishing."

"Ooo, exciting."

"Can you ease up on the sarcasm, Scottie?" my dad said. My parents continued to call me Scottie, like I was five years old.

"Yeah, you're becoming a real bore," Mike added.

I stuck my tongue out at him. "Shut up."

"I can't believe you're heading off to college in the fall." My mother attempted to lighten my mood.

Reminding me I was going away to college wouldn't make me feel better. I was already missing my friends and my home. Although the

Rochester Institute of Technology wasn't too far away, it wasn't home, and my anxiety got in my way sometimes. I liked my house and my bed and everything else in my room, and I feared what awaited me at college.

"Time goes by too fast. Before we know it, you'll be graduating from college, then getting married and having children of your own."

"Geez, Mom, I don't even have a girlfriend." Nothing my mother said made me feel better, especially since she brought up the whole girlfriend thing or lack thereof. Too focused on school and sports, I was never one to keep a steady girlfriend.

"I didn't say you'd be getting married right now. I said someday."

"Okay, someday." I closed my eyes, resting my head against the window. Slouched in my seat, I wished for sleep as my parent's continued their annoying conversation.

"And Mike will be starting high school."

"Let's not rush things," my dad said. "He's only in junior high."

"I know, but he's getting so big." My mother went on and on, recounting every milestone in her two sons' lives, stories I'd heard dozens of times.

Finally, much appreciated sleep came. The next time I opened my eyes, I found Mike hovering over me, squeezing my nose, the car no longer moving. With Mike's fingers pinching my nostrils, I realized we were parked in a makeshift gravel parking lot.

"Get off me, fungus," I said to Mike, who had been squeezing my nose for years, annoying the hell out of me. I used to think it was the funniest thing ever. Now, at nearly eighteen, I thought it was the most annoying thing in the world, and he only did it to get a rise out of me.

In front of us was a rustic log-cabin style multi-level house, surrounded by a series of cottages. Beyond the cottages was a lake, tranquil at the moment, as the rain subsided. Outside the main house was a sign that read, *Lachance Inn and Cottages since 1940: No Vacancy.*

"I hear this is a popular place," my mother said. "Look. It says no vacancy."

"Yeah, I can read," I grumbled.

"God, I haven't been here since I was a kid," my dad mused, opening the car door, beaming with nostalgia. "Frankie's parents used to let us have an entire cottage for a week."

A tall, slender man—about my dad's age—stepped out of the main house. He stood on the front stoop, waving at the guests who just pulled into the parking lot. He was no doubt the one and only Frankie Lachance. For a fifty-year-old man, his hair hadn't gone gray. An aging hippie, his light brown hair was longer than most men his age. Long, scraggly curls flew wildly in the post-rain air.

Unlike Frankie, my dad was straight-laced, his salt and pepper hair short and groomed to perfection. My parents resembled a happily married couple right out of a 1950s television sit-com.

In child-like excitement, Frankie skipped a few steps on his way to our station wagon. While I continued to sit in the backseat, I watched the two men hug like long lost friends. As a woman with long, graying hair emerged, my mother got out and walked around the car to greet Frankie and Susan Lachance.

The Lachances were the hugging-type. I sat there amused at the sight because my mother wasn't a hugger, too afraid to wrinkle her clothes. Under these circumstances, she tolerated it, desperate to make a good first impression.

Standing to the right of Susan Lachance, a young man smiled, his hair lighter, straighter, and longer than Frankie's. His dirty blond locks hung an inch or two above his chin, which continuously flopped over his face every time he tucked strands behind his ears. I found it comical, but I wasn't in the mood to laugh or smile. His eyes were as big as his mother's, the same grayish blue. He first hugged my dad, then my mother.

As everyone made their way to the back of the station wagon, I remained in my seat. The young man tapped on the window, startling me. He pointed to the back of the station wagon, urging me to get out and help. Mike had already gotten out of the car, eager to unpack and explore. With an annoyed sigh, I got out to face the music. I hated meeting new people.

"You must be Scott," Frankie Lachance said, shaking my hand enthusiastically. He was way too happy and energetic for my liking. "This is my son, Terry. I bet you boys are around the same age."

"Not quite," my dad said. "Scottie just graduated from high school. Isn't Terry in college?"

"A senior at the University of Vermont," Frankie said proudly.

"Scottie's going to the Rochester Institute of Technology," my dad bragged.

Terry nudged my arm, encouraging me to help unload the station wagon, rescuing me at the same time.

"Call me Scott," I muttered to Terry as I pulled out my duffel bag.

"Call me Terry," he said in a hopeless attempt to be funny and witty.

I slung my duffle bag over my shoulder and picked up my mother's suitcases before following Terry into the inn. My mother must have packed every single pair of shoes she owned. One small suitcase alone held her cosmetics.

"Is your mother planning on moving in?" Terry laughed as I lugged the suitcases up the front steps.

"She never travels light," I said.

Mike trailed behind us, carrying a soccer ball, bat and baseball mitt, his knapsack filled to the brim and heavy on his back. The three of us headed through the entrance hall, toward a back staircase. I was stupid to think there'd be an elevator. By the time we reached the top of the winding wooden staircase, I could barely breathe, overcome with exhaustion.

"Almost there." Terry led us down a hall and to a room that was no bigger than my bedroom at home. The room held two twin beds, one dresser, and two nightstands. I was surprised there was a bathroom in the room.

"I can't believe I'm stuck here all summer," I moaned, looking around the room I'd be forced to share with Mike.

"It's not so bad," Terry said. "I've lived here my whole life and survived."

"Where's the TV?" I asked.

"There isn't one."

"What a way to spend my birthday." I claimed the bed by the window.

"He thinks he's special because he turns eighteen tomorrow," Mike said.

"That's a pretty big birthday," Terry said. "Have anything planned?"

"I'm here," I stated flatly as Mike dumped the contents of his knapsack all over his bed.

"I think you'll have fun here," Terry said. "Well, I have to get to work. I'll see you guys later."

My eyes followed Terry out the door, hoping he was right. As I dropped my bag on my bed, rain came down in buckets again. I hated rain, which contributed to my bad mood. Lying on my bed, the image of Terry Lachance and his warm, welcoming smile popped in my head. If I saw that smile every day, then maybe this summer wouldn't be so bad.

2

Chapter 2

By seven the following morning, the rain had stopped, and the guests were already up and about. Getting up at seven at the end of June was pure hell. I was used to getting up at ten or eleven, not at the butt crack of dawn.

"Wake up, Scottie!" Mike shouted in my ear. "Come on, Scottie, I'm starving."

"I'm coming," I grumbled. "Leave me alone. And stop calling me Scottie, you dipshit."

Since I was a little kid, my parents made a big deal about me and Mike's birthdays. I had no reason to believe this birthday would be any different from previous birthdays. In fact, I expected an even bigger celebration this year, like a big "Happy Birthday!" with a banner, balloons and streamers, embarrassing the hell out of me. My mother usually did some corny thing with my pancakes and bacon, like placing pieces of bacon on my plate in the shape of numbers. Last summer she made me Belgian waffles with a mound of strawberries and whipped cream with two candles on it: a one and a seven. This year was a big year for me, as I was now legally an adult.

In the inn's crowded dining room, I found my parents and Frankie

Lachance sipping their cups of coffee, half-empty breakfast plates in front of them. At an adjacent table, Susan refilled a pot of coffee while Frankie and Susan's son, Terry, removed an empty tray of sausage at the breakfast bar, replacing it with a fresh tray.

What the hell's going on? I wondered, scanning the restaurant. Where were the balloons and streamers? Or my special breakfast? *This can't be happening.*

"Good morning, sweetheart," my mother said to me. "Did you sleep well?"

Despite my brother's snoring and the crickets chirping outside my window, I slept unusually well. "Uh, yeah." The innkeeper's son distracted me. He disappeared through the double doors to the kitchen.

"There's a lovely breakfast buffet over there," my mother said.

"Yes, please help yourself," Frankie said.

Annoyed and hurt, I went to the buffet table with Mike trailing behind me. I would have settled for a simple "Happy Birthday." Instead, I got nothing, this important birthday completely forgotten.

"Good morning," Terry said, re-emerging from the kitchen with a tray of hot bacon, just as perky as his old man.

"How many pieces of sausage can I have?" Mike asked. "And how many pieces of bacon?"

"As many as you want," Terry said. "I haven't had a piece of meat since I was fifteen, but I still love the smell of bacon."

"Why don't you eat meat?" Mike asked.

"He's a vegetarian, dummy," I said.

"Why?" Mike asked again, as if vegetarianism was a new and foreign concept.

"I just don't."

"That's weird," Mike said.

I nodded, agreeing with my kid brother as I helped myself to three sausages and five pieces of bacon. As an athlete and someone with a fast metabolism—or so my mother said—I never had to worry about my weight.

"But you don't mind cooking meat?" I asked, adding a raspberry cheese danish to my plate before moving on to the scrambled eggs.

"Nah. It never bothered me."

While Terry sorted out the bacon, I scooped up some scrambled eggs. With my plate full of food, I headed back to my table.

"Hey," Terry said to me.

I stopped to face him, vaguely interested in what he had to say.

"Happy birthday, Scott."

Impressed he remembered my birthday, I half-smiled. "Thanks," I muttered. How did a complete stranger remember my birthday but my family didn't?

A few minutes into my breakfast, the conversation turned to me but not about my forgotten birthday. "Terry would be happy to take you boys out on the lake," Frankie said. "We have canoes, rowboats, and a motorboat. I hear Mike's eager to go water skiing. It's tricky at first, but you're both young. I bet you'll figure it out in no time."

"The game's on at one," I said.

"Oh, come on," my dad said. "It's a beautiful day out. Are you telling me you can't miss one game?"

If I was home, doing what I wanted to do on my own terms, I wouldn't have had a problem missing a game, but I was here against my will and planned on fighting every suggestion anyone made. "I'll think about it. Maybe after the game."

"And what are you going to do between now and one o'clock?" my mother asked.

"Read or something."

"Read?" Mike said incredulously. "You're going to read? It's summer. You're so weird."

"That's enough, you two." My mother sensed a full-blown argument brewing. "There's nothing wrong with reading. It'd be nice to see you read outside, though. That's what *I'm* going to do."

I pictured my mother sprawled out on a lounge chair by the lake, donned in a pair of designer sunglasses, a white wine spritzer in one hand and a book in her other hand, her make-up still intact.

"Maybe tomorrow," I mumbled.

"It's always tomorrow with you," my dad said.

My dad was right; I was a gifted procrastinator. But this was my summer vacation, and I didn't have to do what people wanted me or expected me to do. After my lumberjack breakfast, I retreated to my room while Mike went somewhere with our dad and the Lachance men.

Sulking in my barren room, I sat on my bed, leaning on the windowsill, admiring the massive trees and cottages. Families shared picnics on the benches, smoke coming from the nearby barbecue grills, even as early as eleven in the morning. Farther away, canoes or kayaks drifted on the lake. I didn't know the difference between the two since I'd never been on either.

Instead of reading, I dug out a sketchbook from my duffel bag and sat by the window. Despite everything, I couldn't deny the fact that the area was beautiful; picturesque, like a postcard. Before we left Massachusetts, I followed my mother's suggestion and packed my watercolors and pastels.

Still full from breakfast, I skipped lunch and continued to hide out in my room, finishing my sketch that was almost ready for my oil pastels, listening to the game on the radio. Too enthralled in my drawing, I didn't hear the knock on my door.

"You can watch the game downstairs," Terry said. "In the lounge."

Unnerved by the audacity of him opening my door without permission, I was at a loss for words.

"You left your door open. I wouldn't just walk in on you."

"I'm fine here." I returned to my drawing.

"I was told to come and get you and be a good host. Our parents assume we'll automatically get along because we're close in age, but they're wrong. I can see we're nothing alike."

"How do you know we're nothing alike? You've never met me before."

"For one, you like sports. Football? Soccer? You're listening to the Red Sox. I bet you play baseball, too."

"Yeah, I played."

"And you're a city kid. As you can see, I'm not."

"I'm not a kid," I corrected him.

"And I bet if I asked you what you do for fun, you'll say girls, right?"

"Wrong." Fed up with Terry's assumptions about me, I just wanted to be alone and draw. "I'm sort of busy, so if you don't mind..."

"Okay, I'm leaving." But he didn't leave. Instead, he took a few steps toward me, trying to get a peek at my drawing. "Are you an artist?"

"Yeah, a bit."

"I like to draw and paint, too."

"I paint a little, too." I nodded toward my tubes of paint on my bed.

"Maybe we have one thing in common."

"You didn't think a sporty guy like me could draw, right? That I wasn't the type to draw or paint, is that it?"

"I apologize for making such an assumption. I've been working at it. I guess I better keep trying."

"Working at what?"

"Not being so judgmental or presumptuous," he said, his eyes on my sketchbook. "It's very good. I love how you captured the two toddlers. They're twins, you know. Your attention to detail is incredible."

Without my permission, he sat on my bed and took my sketchbook from me, again without my permission, but I didn't protest because he seemed genuinely interested in my artistic capabilities. "Oh, wow." He examined the drawing I did a few weeks ago while spending the afternoon alone in the Arboretum. "I wish I could draw trees like you."

"Trees are nothing. I wish I could draw people."

"You do."

"Mine are more like Monet's. I wish I could draw portraits or figures, but I guess everybody has a niche. What's yours?"

"Portraits and figures." He glanced up at me with his smiling, big gray-blue eyes. Terry flipped through each drawing I crammed into my over-sized sketchbook. With my eyes on him, I stopped paying attention to the ballgame, focusing instead on Terry. For someone who lived out here in the sticks, he was sort of interesting.

"What do you plan on studying at Rochester Tech?" he asked.

"Design," I replied, as if he should have already known that.

"Yeah, I guess that's why you're going to Rochester Tech, right? I think you'd be very good at it. Your dad's in design, right?"

"Sort of. He's a senior partner in an advertising firm in Boston."

"Are you planning on following in his footsteps?"

"No. I don't want to work a hundred hours a week." My dad was on his way to working himself to death, a fate I didn't want to replicate. Although I was usually too nervous or flat out not interested in asking a lot of questions of people, I didn't hesitate with Terry because he piqued my curiosity. "What do you study at the University of Vermont?"

"Sociology and Economics."

"Ooo, interesting," I said in my usual sarcastic tone. Both subjects seemed boring to me.

"I'm joining the Peace Corps after I graduate. My parents count on me in the summer, but they want me to go. As much as I love this place, I need to go out and do something on my own."

"That's cool," I said, envious that he had the guts to do something adventurous and meaningful. "I don't think I could do anything like that."

"Why not?"

"I get homesick when I'm gone for more than a night. Don't tell anyone I said that."

"Are you homesick right now?"

I shrugged, not entirely sure.

"Is that why you're being antisocial?"

"I'm not antisocial," I insisted. "I just don't want to be here."

"It's not so bad. You might as well make the most of it. I can show you how to water ski. The lake's nice, too; not too cold."

Everyone assumed I'd like water skiing. Maybe I would, but I convinced myself I'd never get the hang of it and fall flat on my face. I didn't want to make a complete fool of myself.

"Or tubing," he added. "You and Mike could sit in the tube and I'll pull you along. It's a lot of fun. Or you could drive the boat and I'll water ski."

Driving the boat intrigued me, but the worst scenario came to mind: what if I crashed into the dock or another boat or canoe? What if I lost control, smashing into one of the surrounding trees? I didn't want to kill anybody, including myself.

"Maybe some other time, huh?" He closed my sketchbook after I didn't respond. "Well, I better go. I have to do some gardening. I suppose you don't want to help?" He paused, waiting for my answer that wouldn't come. I hadn't gardened a day in my life, and it didn't particularly appeal to me. "Just joking. Gardening's one of my least favorite jobs. You might make it more interesting."

"There's nothing interesting about me." I wondered why in the world he thought I'd "make it more interesting."

"Maybe not." He got up to leave. "But you're a bit of a novelty to me."

A novelty?

"I mostly hang out with kids and their parents and grandparents," he explained. "You're not like most guests here. You're different and I like different." He hesitated before leaving. "Are you sure you don't want to come down? I bet I could scrounge up a piece of cake in the kitchen."

"No, thanks," I said, although tempted to go with him.

"How about a beer? I guess it's a little too early for a beer. Maybe later."

Confused with his intent, like he had some underlying motive, I didn't know how to respond. Why was this stranger being so nice to me? "I'd like to see your artwork." I surprised myself with a sudden change in subject.

"You would?"

"Yes. Where's your room?" I hoped he'd forgo his gardening duties to spend more time with me.

"I sleep in one of the cottages, but it's way too nice to be cooped up inside, so maybe some other time. Enjoy being miserable inside. Just don't let life pass you by."

Don't let life pass me by? At only eighteen, I had no intention of letting life pass me by and resented Terry's comment. I didn't want to admit he was a little right since I often avoided new situations and places.

For the next hour, I contemplated turning off the radio and tracking Mike down. Peering out my window, my eyes gravitated toward Terry as he knelt in a flowerbed, pulling out the weeds. In old, ragged jean shorts, he didn't seem to care or notice that people could see his butt crack. My eyes followed him from one flower bed to another. Occasionally he'd stand up, talking to a guest or two. He smiled a lot. And why shouldn't he? He had perfectly straight white teeth with a smile that was both warm and infectious, one that could make me smile. At one point, he waved up at my window as if he had been eyeing me, too.

After a losing Red Sox game, I was both annoyed and starving, more annoyed because I was so hungry and not because the Red Sox lost. Responding to my hunger pangs, I left the safety of my room. It was almost dinnertime, anyway.

At five o'clock, I expected to find my family in the dining room, but they weren't there, so I searched for them outside. Within seconds, Mike spotted me and ran toward me in his swimsuit, dripping wet. "We're having a cookout," he said, out of breath. "We're over there." He pointed to a picnic table by the lake where my parents and Frankie and Susan Lachance sat. Terry was at the charcoal grill in his bare feet, changed and showered, wearing baggy jeans and a red t-shirt, holding a spatula.

"Hi, sweetheart," my mother said as I approached the picnic bench, instantly embarrassing me in front of Terry and his parents.

"Aren't you a vegetarian?" I asked Terry, sitting down across from my parents.

"Yeah, but he doesn't mind cooking," Susan answered on Terry's behalf. "He made himself a veggie burger."

"You should have one," his father said, pointing to a plate beside the potato salad. They looked just like regular burgers. "He makes them from scratch."

"No, thanks. I like meat."

Terry placed a plateful of hamburgers and hot dogs in the middle of the table. Of all places to sit, he sat beside me. As he scooped some potato salad onto his paper plate, I sat there frozen like a dummy, watching everyone indulge themselves on burgers and hot dogs.

"Aren't you hungry, Scottie?" my mother asked.

I wished everyone would stop calling me Scottie.

"Yeah, you better eat before Mike eats everything," my dad added.

With Terry sitting beside me, I didn't want to make a slob of myself. For some unknown reason, my hand shook as I reached for the potato salad.

"Terry plays guitar," Mike said with a mouthful of hot dog.

"Don't talk with your mouth full," my mother reprimanded him.

"He's playing in the pub tonight," Mike said, swallowing his food. "Mom and Dad said I can stay up to watch."

"Where's the pub?" I asked.

"Right off the dining room," Frankie said.

"We opened it a few years ago after a guest complained there was nothing for the adults to do in the evening," Susan interjected.

"On Saturday nights we turn the dining room into a dance hall," Frankie explained. "But guests wanted more."

"And the dances are for old people," Terry said.

"They're not for old people," Susan said. "Just because you don't dance."

"They're for old people," Terry said to me. "They play waltzes and shit like that."

"Please watch your language," Susan said. "There are children present."

I hoped she was referring to Mike and not me.

"It sounds like fun," my mother said.

Going to the pub and listening to Terry play seemed more fun to me than dancing with a bunch of "old people."

After gorging ourselves on hamburgers, hot dogs, and potato salad, Mike, Terry, and I still had room for s'mores. Mike and I had three each while Terry had one. By that point, I was so full I was ready for a nap but fought off the temptation and went to the pub with everyone else, looking forward to my first beer as a legitimate adult. My parents were too busy socializing with the Lachances and people around them to notice I ordered a beer, eagerly waiting to hear Terry perform.

"What are you doing with that beer?" my dad asked, discovering my half-finished pint of beer.

"I'm eighteen," I pointed out. "I can have a beer if I want one."

"Oh, shit. We forgot your birthday, didn't we?"

Across from me, my mother gabbed to a woman at the adjacent table, a woman I had never seen before in my life. A gifted socializer, my mother would talk to anybody willing to listen.

"Nancy," my dad raised his voice over the crowded pub.

Meanwhile, I sat there with my beer, watching Terry tune his acoustic guitar in the corner of the pub. I looked forward to hearing him play.

"Nancy." He finally got her attention. "Did you know it's Scottie's birthday today?"

"It's not his..." She stopped, realizing the tremendous mistake she made by forgetting her oldest son's birthday. My cheeks burned in both annoyance and embarrassment. "Oh, my goodness," she gasped. "What day is it?"

"June twenty-ninth," I stated.

"Oh, my gosh." She got up to hug me. "I'm so sorry. I've never forgotten a birthday in my life. Maybe I didn't want to believe my baby's growing up."

Ugh. I brought my pint to my lips.

"And here you are, drinking a beer like a grownup," she went on, continuing to embarrass me. "We'll make it up to you. What kind of cake would you like? Maybe the restaurant here could..."

I stopped listening to my mother as Terry started to play. My embarrassment grew as Terry opened with *Happy Birthday.* Slouched in my seat, I gulped down the rest of my beer, ready for another. If it wasn't so dark in the pub, everyone would have discovered a very red Thomas Scott Prescott.

3

Chapter 3

Mesmerized with the bare-footed Terry Lachance, I listened intently as he plucked the opening riff of Simon and Garfunkel's *The Boxer*. All I wanted to do was drink beer and listen to Terry without my parents babbling nonsense. Terry had a nice voice and didn't play too badly, either. I could have listened to him all night.

"He's a good kid," my dad said. "Frankie tells me he's joining the Peace Corps."

I wish he'd shut up so I can listen in peace.

"That's such a Lachance thing to do," my dad continued. "The family's full of bleeding heart liberals." If people didn't conform to my dad's conservative views, then he considered them "bleeding heart liberals." He thought Nixon was the greatest president ever, not bothered by the Watergate scandal. To him, President Carter was the worst.

Terry smiled often, singing and playing guitar to this small audience, happy and carefree. I wished I was more like him instead of anxious and miserable for unknown reasons.

Disinterested in Terry, my mother yawned, a telltale sign she wouldn't stay much longer. Mike, too, yawned, his eyes heavy. He was probably the youngest guest in the pub.

"Are you sure you're okay to stay down here by yourself?" my mother asked me, as if I couldn't take care of myself.

"I'll be fine," I assured her.

"Aww, but won't you be lonely?"

"No. I'm fine. Go to bed. I'll see you in the morning."

"Okay, honey."

I rolled my eyes as she kissed me goodnight, just like a little boy.

As Terry played his Simon and Garfunkel favorites, I downed two more beers, working on my third when he took a break. After ordering a beer at the bar, he headed toward me at my vacant table. "Is it okay if I sit here?" he asked.

My heart raced and I stopped breathing, as if I was about to have a panic attack, which was weird considering I had grown accustomed to my surroundings. Before I had the chance to respond, Terry was already sitting beside me.

"It's good to see you out of your room," he said.

"I've been out of my room since dinner."

"That's good." As he took a sip of his beer, pieces of his dirty blond hair flopped over his eyes. Biting on his bottom lip, he tucked those strands behind his ears. Once again, I stopped breathing, bats or something flapping around in my stomach.

"Do you play here every night?" I asked after exhaling quietly.

"No. What'd you think? Pretty bad, huh?"

"No, it's not bad." I liked the way he sang. "Do you take requests?"

"What do you have in mind? I could sing an encore of *Happy Birthday*?" He looked straight at me. Half smiling, he tucked his hair behind his ears, his cheeks a light shade of pink.

"God no, please don't. How about *Yesterday* or *Blackbird*? But you can play whatever you want. I don't care." *Blackbird* was one of my favorite songs, and I looked forward to hearing him play it.

"I can play *Blackbird.*" He stood up, gulping down his pint of beer at the same time. He smiled at me on his way to his corner stool. Occasionally I'd shift in my seat, taking a sip of beer as his eyes met mine. Terry played a few more folksy songs before calling it quits for the night. He returned to my table with two shot glasses and a bottle of whiskey.

"What's this?" I asked as he handed me a shot.

"Tequila."

"I've never had tequila before." After finishing my third beer, I had a buzz. I had only gotten drunk three times in my life, and this would be my fourth.

"Happy birthday," he said, clinking his shot glass with mine. Simultaneously, we chugged ours down. I instantly coughed, the tequila burning my throat. "Here, suck on this." He laughed, handing me a lime. "I forgot the salt. You're supposed to lick, drink, then suck."

Despite my throat burning and subsequent coughing, I poured myself another shot and picked up the salt shaker in the middle of the table. "What do I do with it?"

"Here, let me show you." He reached for my hand. Taking the salt shaker from me, he shook some salt on the top of my hand. He scanned the pub, making sure we were alone. The bartender was too busy cleaning up to notice us. Terry brought my hand to his mouth and licked the salt off it. My heart beat out of my chest, enjoying his tongue along my skin. He released my hand and chugged down his shot of tequila, ending the sequence by sticking a piece of lime in his mouth.

"Let me try," I said, reaching for his hand. I straightened out his hand, admiring his long fingers. After shaking some salt on his palm, I didn't hesitate, dragging my tongue along it, licking him clean. If given the chance, I would have done more than lick the salt. His giggles made me want to do it again and again.

Our eyes met as I brought the shot glass to my lips. I didn't cough this time and couldn't wait to do another. After two more rounds, I staggered to my feet, nearly falling over.

"Whoa," Terry said, standing up, steadying me.

"I wanna go swimming," I slurred. "Come with me."

"Okay, let's go, birthday boy." He left the shot glasses on the table, taking only the tequila bottle.

I leaned against Terry on the way out of the pub and into the dark night. Dim lights flickered in the distant cottages, but most of the scarce light came from the stars in the sky. By the lake, I stripped down to my underwear. The shy and nervous type, I wouldn't have done anything like this if I had been sober.

"Are you coming or what?" I asked.

"I'm coming." He took off his t-shirt.

Although thinner than I—maybe even a little skinny— his arms were slightly muscular and toned from all the yard work and gardening he did. I had more of an athletic build. In my drunkenness, I ran into the water as Terry fell over, attempting to take off his jeans.

"Hey," I called to him. "You need any help?"

"Nah, I got it." He kicked off his jeans. In his boxers, he ran into the water, trudging toward me. We swam all the way to the dock, planning to lie on top of it to admire the stars. However, I was too drunk to climb on top, so I swam back to land. I took a swig of the tequila, plopping down on the grass. Terry did the same, lying beside me.

"It's not so bad here," I said, staring up into the starry night as we lay on our backs.

"Why do you think I still live here? You're a good swimmer... even drunk." Terry sat up, having his turn with the bottle of tequila. "I rarely drink. I have a feeling I'll regret it in the morning."

In my attempt to stand up, I burst into laughter as I fell back down, landing on my back. Terry staggered to his feet. Grabbing both my hands, he hauled me up. Everything was spinning out of control. Three

Terry Lachances stood in front of me and each of them was as good looking as the other. "Do you have a girlfriend?" I asked, my speech slurred more than before.

"No." He held my shoulders so I wouldn't topple over.

"Hmm," I grunted. "That's too bad because..." I lost my train of thought as the spinning grew more and more intense.

"Scott, are you okay?" Terry squeezed my bare shoulders.

As I took a step toward him, I did the worst thing imaginable: I bent over and threw up, splattering vomit all over Terry's bare feet. Hunched over, more and more vomit poured out of me. I just wanted to die.

And then I thought I really did.

4

Chapter 4

Nothing was worse than waking up with the taste of vomit in my mouth, together with a headache that pierced the center of my brain. *I'm going to die*, I thought. I lay in bed with the blankets over my head, protecting myself from the burning sun. As I opened my eyes, I discovered I wasn't in my room. The sun painfully blinded me as I pushed the blankets down to my shoulders. I spotted Terry standing by a window, folding clothes.

"Hey there," he said. "How's your head?"

"Oh, my God," I muttered, holding my throbbing head, recalling the events of last night, most notably me puking my guts out all over Terry. "Did I throw up on you?"

"Yeah, but it's okay. It's not like I haven't done it before. Just not on anyone else."

"Oh, God," I groaned again.

Terry smirked, carrying on with what he was doing. "Don't worry about it. You can take a shower here and borrow some clothes. You stink. I can smell you from here."

"Yeah, like your clothes would fit me." I swung my legs over the side of the bed. My eyes wandered around the room as I sat on Terry's queen-sized bed. I held the blankets up to my chin, shielding my half-naked body from Terry's prying eyes. Across the room, a small couch sat in front of a fireplace with a bookcase and acoustic guitar in the corner, proving this was Terry's room. "I don't think I'll ever drink again." Collapsing back in the bed, I pulled the blankets over my head. As I hid from the world again, the mattress sunk to one side.

"My head hurts, too," Terry said, tugging down the blanket, exposing the top half of my head. "But I had fun. Maybe we can do it again sometime." He paused before continuing. "Without the tequila. Your family's probably wondering where you are. You want me to get you some breakfast?"

"Are you kidding me? I can't eat like this."

"How about some coffee? I'll bring you back a cup if you want. You can stay here and recover."

"No, thanks." I had never been so hung over in my entire life. *Never again*, I told myself. Terry left, allowing me to sleep off my hangover in his bed.

After a lengthy sleep, I felt somewhat recovered. Alone in Terry's cottage at three in the afternoon, I discovered he had washed and folded my clothes, leaving them on the edge of his bed. Bleary-eyed, I returned to my room to brush my teeth and rinse my mouth with mouthwash.

Down by the lake, Terry and Mike sat in a rowboat while my mother dozed on a lounge chair, soaking up the late afternoon sun. I smiled as Terry waved at me.

"Hi, sweetheart." My mother startled me. I thought she was asleep. "Are you feeling better?"

"Uh... yeah," I said, distracted by Terry in the boat as he made his way back to the bank of the lake.

"You must be hungry," my mother continued. "You've eaten nothing all day."

"Yeah, I guess I'm a little hungry." A tray of watermelon on the table caught my eye. I grabbed the biggest slice, then turned around so Terry wouldn't see me dribble and make a mess of myself.

"Where have you been?" Mike demanded. "Terry took me tubing. You should've come."

"I was sick."

"What are you doing now?" Terry asked me.

I wiped my mouth with the back of my hand and turned around to face Terry. Judging by his sunburnt nose, he must have spent most of the day outside in the sun. My stomach squirmed as he smiled at me. Were those butterflies in my stomach or had the bats returned?

"Uh... um... nothing, I guess."

"Come on, I'll take you rowing."

"You don't have to," my mother said to Terry. "You must be tired. My boys know how to entertain themselves."

"I'm not tired," Terry said. "I don't mind." He stepped back into the boat, his eyes on me. "Let's go, Scott," he said. It was more like a command.

"Fine. I'm coming, I'm coming."

"Have you ever rowed before?" he asked as we sat on opposite ends of the boat.

"No."

"Wanna give it a go?"

"Sure." Rowing was a lot harder than it looked. At least three times, I lost my grasp, rescuing the oars before they floated away. Although I was an athlete in high school and strong enough to row, I still fumbled with the oars, unable to get the hang of it. "How do you do it with your little arms?" I asked, frustrated that we weren't going anywhere.

"They might not be as big as yours, but I wouldn't call them little," he responded, examining his arms.

Leaning over, I squeezed his bicep, almost losing the oars again. His bicep was slender yet solid. As I squeezed, his cheeks turned as pink as his nose. "Okay, so they're not so little."

"Now hand over the oars before they float away." Taking over, he rowed for about fifteen more minutes, stopping at the far end of the lake, a secluded area with no houses, picnic benches, or signs of civilization. "I come here a lot when I want to be alone. My dad used to bring me here all the time when I was a kid, when we wanted to get away from everyone. Come on, let's go for a swim. It's your chance to prove you're just as fun sober."

I didn't expect Terry to strip naked. As he shed his clothes, I looked away. "What the hell are you doing?" I asked, diverting my eyes. He folded his clothes neatly and placed them in the boat.

"What? Haven't you gone skinny dipping before?"

"No." I vehemently shook my head.

"You really haven't lived, have you? I promise you, no one comes out here." He waited for me to take off my clothes but gave up after thirty seconds. "Fine. Suit yourself." He turned and ran into the lake. As he ran, I admired his cute little ass. Ashamed of my abnormal and disgusting thoughts, I nevertheless couldn't stop looking.

On this hot summer day, the water was inviting, especially as I watched Terry splashing and having a blast. Surrendering to temptation, I turned around and undressed. Naked, I sprinted into the water. Terry smirked, proud that he convinced me to skinny dip with him. As I approached him, he disappeared under the water, swimming away.

Terry was a bundle of energy, running out of the water and to a tree where a rope hung from a limb. "My dad put this up when I was a kid. I still use it."

"You probably weigh about the same as you did then," I joked.

"You think you're so funny, don't you?"

I continued to stand in the water while Terry jumped up on the rope. He kicked off, swinging over the water, letting go a few inches in front of me. "Go on. Try it. I know you want to."

Although tempted, I shook my head.

"Come on. I'll help you." He grabbed my arm and coaxed me out of the water. As he held the rope with one hand, he reached for my waist with the other.

I swallowed hard, taking the rope from him. As I jumped on it, Terry gave me one big push. Instead of letting go, I swung back to him. Both laughing hysterically, Terry pushed again, laughing harder as I bounced back again. For the final time, Terry jumped on my back, and the two of us swung over the water. The rope proved to be as strong as Terry said it was. I got out of the water and swung from the rope again. As much as I liked Terry on my back, I did it alone this time.

We stayed out there until the sun faded. I didn't want to go back. I wanted to stay out there with this guy I just met three days ago. We shared a weird connection that confused the hell out of me. Different from anyone I'd ever met, he was as much of a novelty to me as I was to him.

"What are you doing later?" I asked, watching his slim figure bend over to pick up his t-shirt. He hesitated before putting it on.

"I thought about having a bonfire. The kids love it."

"Do you usually play and sing like a good Boy Scout?" I teased.

"Yes." My snide comment didn't offend him.

I looked forward to hearing him sing and play again, whether it was around a campfire with a bunch of kids or in a country pub. "Cool," I said, getting dressed. Strangely comfortable around Terry, I had almost forgotten I was naked.

Everyone was at the picnic table, waiting for us to return. Ravenous, I would have eaten everything in sight if given the opportunity. "Where have you been?" my nosy brother asked.

"Canoeing," I replied, annoyed that my family had a need to know where I was at all times.

"Rowing," Terry corrected me. "Not canoeing."

"I think it's wonderful that the boys are getting along so well," Susan said.

"I knew he'd come around," my dad said. "Right, Scottie?"

"Whatever," I mumbled, sitting down on the picnic bench. While Terry sat beside me, our knees rubbed together under the table. There was only one piece of corn on the cob left on the platter. I sensed a battle about to ensue over who would get the last piece. Terry snagged it before I got the chance.

As one of the most generous men I'd ever met in my life, Terry placed the last piece of corn on a plate and passed it to me.

5

Chapter 5

During the bonfire activities, Mike and I roasted marshmallow after marshmallow while Terry played his guitar, leading people in corny campfire songs. Every once in a while, I'd catch Terry smiling in my direction. His entire face lit up when he smiled. Mike and I repeatedly shoved our gooey, sticky fingers in each other's faces, acting like two bratty kids. In typical Mike fashion, he got carried away, smearing my nose with melted chocolate. I pushed his shoulders so hard he stumbled backwards.

"Stop it, you two," my mother scolded us.

"I didn't do anything," Mike insisted.

"Look what he did to me," I said, pointing to my chocolate-covered face.

"Michael, go to your room," my mother said.

"But..." he whined.

"You heard your mother," my dad said, fed up with our childish antics. "Go now."

"How come Scottie doesn't have to go?"

"Stop calling me Scottie," I said through gritted teeth, about to push him again.

"You both need a break from each other," my mother said. "Now go, Michael. I won't tell you again."

Mike stomped his feet, begrudgingly leaving. I trudged into the lake to wash the chocolate off my hands and face. Once cleaned, I sat on the grass as everyone dispersed for the night. I wasn't ready to go to bed. As I gazed into the lake, footsteps grew closer and closer. *It's him*, I thought. My heart raced and my hands turned clammy.

"Nice night, huh?" Terry said, sitting down beside me. He brought his knobby knees to his chest, resting his head on top of them, turning his head toward me. He had kind, honest, and penetrating eyes that could see through me.

"It's weird, but I feel like I've known you forever," I said.

With his arms wrapped around his knees, he rocked himself subtly, his eyes still on me. Maybe he felt the same way about me. Terry's silence caught me off guard.

"I know I'm weird. Mike says I'm weird."

"Since when do you listen to your brother?" He placed a hand on my shoulder. "Besides, being weird isn't so bad." He rubbed his thumb back and forth against my shoulder. I wished I wasn't wearing a t-shirt so I'd feel his thumb on my bare skin. Those familiar butterflies fluttered in my stomach.

"I'd like to see your artwork. What are you doing now?"

Smiling, he withdrew his hand, shifting his gaze to the lake. "It's late and I'm kind of wiped. Maybe tomorrow?"

"Okay." Although disappointed, I'd settle for tomorrow. I longed for him to touch my shoulder again. He didn't budge, though, continuing to hold his knees against his chest. I didn't want to say goodnight, but we had to go to bed at some point.

* * *

Ready to start the day at seven, eager to see Terry, I was the first one down for breakfast. I found him at the buffet table, loading a basket with freshly baked bread. "Good morning," he said with a smile. "You're up early."

"I'm hungry." While I was starving, I was more hungry for Terry.

"Do you like waffles? You can make your own. Come, let me show you. The batter's fresh. I made it this morning." He walked me to a table with a waffle maker and a tub of batter. "It only takes a minute." He scooped a spoonful of batter into the waffle maker. He made one for me, then one for himself. With our plates of waffles, syrup, strawberries, and whipped cream, we sat at a nearby table, the only ones in the restaurant.

As we ate and talked, guests filtered in. Terry pushed his plate across the table, urging me to finish his half-eaten waffle. "I better get back to work. I'll see you later." Because I had such a ravenous appetite, I had no trouble finishing his plate.

By mid-morning, my family and everyone else had finished their breakfasts and were ready to go. The first thing on the agenda was water tubing. With Frankie at the wheel of the motorboat, Terry, Mike, and I sat in a giant rubber tube. We had a lot of fun, even when Terry and Mike teamed up against me to push me out.

"You're going to pay for that!" I shouted from the water, ready to kill both of them as they laughed at my expense. The motorboat stopped, allowing me to catch up to it. I swam back to them. "You guys think you're so funny."

"Are you all right, son?" Frankie asked me as I clutched the tube, out of breath.

"Yeah, I'm okay."

"How many times have I told you not to push people out?" Frankie reprimanded Terry. "Help him back in."

Terry heaved me back into the tube. As he snickered under his breath, I shoved his arm. "Sorry," Terry said.

"No, you're not," I said, admiring his mischievous grin and playful eyes.

After our tubing adventure, we all settled down for lunch at our usual picnic table. Frankie, my dad, and Mike discussed going fishing in a nearby pond. To me, fishing sounded downright boring. "I don't want to go fishing," I grumbled.

"Then don't go," my dad said. "Entertain yourself. You're good at that."

"We can hang out," Terry suggested. Under the table, his bare foot landed on top of mine. My breathing turned shallow as my cheeks burned. "I'll take you out in the boat again. You need a few more lessons. Is that okay with you?" he asked me, curling his toes over mine. Of course it was okay.

Terry insisted on teaching me how to row, convinced I'd get the hang of it before summer ended. I was just as useless as the day before. I passed the oars to Terry so we'd reach our destination before nightfall. He removed his swimsuit and tossed it in the boat. I didn't look away this time.

"Are you coming?" he asked, standing in front of me. "You don't have to go skinny-dipping if you don't want to. I like it because I can't do it anywhere else, and I don't think I'd do it with anyone else."

Something was happening inside my swimsuit that I didn't want Terry to see, so I stood there, not sure what to do.

"I'll meet you in the water." He backed away from me.

As Terry approached the rope, I had a sudden change of heart. "Wait." As I pushed down my swimsuit, my cock sprung free. I didn't say anything, walking toward Terry, his big gray-blue eyes opening wider. Right when Terry was about to kick off, I ran to him and jumped on his back. Together, we swung from the rope and landed in the lake. I tread water, avoiding Terry until my body was back to normal.

After several more swings, I plopped down on the grass, exhausted, but Terry kept going. "What's the matter with you?" he asked me.

"I need a break."

"A break?" Terry emerged from the lake. "Don't be a bore." Dripping, he hovered over me and shook his hair like a wet, shaggy dog. Abruptly jumping to my feet, I wrapped my arm around his neck, trapping him in a headlock, something I'd done to Mike a million times. With one arm around his neck, I discovered he was ticklish as my fingers brushed against his stomach. He giggled so hard he could barely stand, let alone breathe. That's when I ruthlessly dug my fingers into his sides. We both tumbled to the ground with Terry landing face-first in the grass. I sat on his thighs, pinning him on the ground, continuing to tickle him.

"Truce! Damn, you're vicious."

"I told you you'd pay for what you did." I slapped his bare ass before sprinting into the water.

Terry ran after me, laughing hard. In the water, he jumped on my back and yanked my hair back. Due for a haircut, my hair was longer than usual. Once he released his grasp, I flipped him over my head. He came after me and dunked me under, holding me there until I overpowered him. We fought like this until we thoroughly exhausted ourselves. I trailed behind Terry, contemplating slapping his ass again. Boy, was I messed up.

"Stop looking at my ass," he said.

"Why would I look at your skinny ass?" I teased.

"I don't know." He collapsed on the ground by the boat. "Mike's right; you are weird."

"There's nothing wrong with being weird, right?"

With his legs stretched out in front of him, he closed his eyes. He was the most beautiful thing I'd ever seen in my life.

"Are you just going to stand there and stare at me?" he asked with his eyes closed.

"I'm not staring," I lied, sitting beside him. As he dozed off, various feelings ran through me, feelings that weren't new but stronger than I'd ever had. Ashamed of myself, I scanned his body, loving every inch. As Terry rested his head on my shoulder, my body reacted like it did earlier. My hand gravitated toward his thigh. He stirred as my hand crept farther up his body, landing on his stomach. Half asleep, he smiled into my shoulder.

"Are you going to tickle me again?" he asked sleepily.

"Only if you want me to." I stroked his stomach.

"Nah. Maybe later." He shuddered, inhaling deeply as my fingers brushed against the tufts of light brown hair inches below his belly button. I desperately wanted to touch him. "I'm tired," he yawned but didn't tell me to stop.

"Yes, I can see that." As my hand inched lower, Terry brought his knees to his chest, curling into the fetal position. He leaned against me, finally drifting off to sleep. "I don't know what to do," I whispered, breathing into his hair. "I don't know what to do."

As he slept beside me, my heart beating wildly the whole time, Terry didn't make a sound.

6

Chapter 6

Tonight's idea of fun was going to the local drive-in. *Herbie Goes Bananas* and *Bon Voyage, Charlie Brown* played on one screen and *The Shining* and *Friday the Thirteenth* on the second screen. Despite my propensity for nightmares after watching horror movies, my choice still would have been *The Shining*, but my parents wouldn't let my twelve-year-old brother see a Steven King movie.

In the Lachance family's red Ford pickup truck, Susan sat in the front with Frankie, the driver, while the rest of us hopped in the back, way before seat belts were mandatory. Even my mother sat with us in her denim capris and pink blouse with matching headband. The drive-in proved to be quite the happening place for families. To get a good spot, cars started arriving at six o'clock. We arrived closer to seven but still got a decent spot.

To pass the time while we waited for the sun to go down, Mike and I tossed the football around. Our parents organized their chairs in front of the pickup, making themselves comfortable. A few pieces of popcorn hit the back of my head, distracting me enough that I lost my concentration and the football struck the side of my head.

Meanwhile, Terry sat alone in the back of the pickup, staring straight ahead and not at me. That smirk on his face proved to me he was the culprit who flung the popcorn at me. Tossing the football back to Mike, I went to Terry and sat beside him. I grabbed a handful of popcorn and threw it in his face.

"Stop it," Mike said, running to us as the movie trailers started. "Don't waste all the popcorn."

"Relax," I said. "We have plenty."

As our legs dangled off the side of the truck, Terry's feet bounced against mine, my fingers wiggling back and forth against the side of his thigh. He giggled under his breath. He squeezed his hand between our thighs, placing his hand on top of mine, forcing me to stop wiggling my fingers.

Bored with this stupid kid's movie, Terry and I wandered off, passing the Snack Shack on our way to the second screen. We sat hidden in the back, a clump of trees to the left of us. We could just about see the screen and hear the sounds of the movie coming from the surrounding cars. Propped on my elbows, I lay beside Terry, the palm of his hand planted behind my back, right above my ass. My thoughts turned to his cute ass and how much I couldn't wait to see it again.

"You're not paying attention to the movie," Terry said, leaning into me, resting his chin on my shoulder.

"No, I am," I lied, swallowing hard. "But I don't think you are."

"No, I'm watching." He looked at me instead of the screen.

"Then why are you looking at me?"

"Because I feel like it." He smiled into my shoulder.

After a few minutes of silence, I felt the need to speak. "The last time I went to the drive-in was with Mary Ellen Kelleher, but we weren't interested in the movie. Mary Ellen was too busy going down on me in the backseat."

Did I just tell him that? Embarrassed, I burst into nervous laughter. Even in the dark, I noticed Terry blush. Now I regretted saying it even more. Mary Ellen, the captain of the girls' field hockey team, and I dated on and off for five months. She was the only one I nearly went all the way with. I would have, too, if the rubber hadn't broken. I freaked out and that was the end of our relationship.

Throughout my high school days, I went out with girls and fooled around with them because that's what everyone expected me to do. It's not that I didn't like it; it just wasn't as great as my friends made it out to be. I made it to third base a few times but never scored a home run.

"Did you go to the Prom with her?" he asked. "I assume you went. You know, someone like you."

"Someone like me?" I said, slightly offended. "What does that mean?"

"It means someone like you would go to the Prom because that's what you're supposed to do, right? I bet all your friends went. If you didn't go, your mother would have had a fit. She'd never want to be embarrassed in front of her country club friends, right?"

Terry nailed it, but I didn't want to admit it to him. I went to the Prom with Cathy Bressette, one of the longest and most boring nights of my life. "Did you go?" I asked.

"No. It wasn't really my scene. Maybe I'll see you dance Saturday. We're throwing a party for our dads' birthdays. I'm sure there are a few teen girls who would love to dance with you."

"I don't know about that. You're the one with the dreamy blue eyes," I teased him.

Shaking his head, he looked away from me. "I'm not much of a dancer. I'd probably step on their toes and they'd never want to come back again."

Instead of watching the movie, Terry continued to ask questions. The movie was the farthest thing from our minds. "So, I have another question for you," he said, bringing his arm around my waist. Butterflies fluttered in my stomach as the hair on the back of my neck stuck up.

"If you could go anywhere in the world, where would you go?"

"Hmm... " I thought for a minute. "Hawaii, I guess. You?"

"I always wanted to go backpacking across India."

"Maybe the Peace Corps will send you there."

"I doubt it. They're probably going to send me to Africa or South America." He paused, thinking of what to ask next. "Do you want to get married?"

"That's a bit personal."

"Come on, answer." He was practically pleading. "Do you?"

"I guess I want to get married... someday."

"Kids?"

"I think so." My family expected me to settle down with a wife and kids. "How about you? Do you want—"

"There you are!" Mike exclaimed. Terry instantly withdrew his arm. "You're not supposed to be over here."

"We were bored," I said, standing up.

"You better go back before you get in trouble," Mike said.

Terry and I trailed behind Mike as he led the way back to the pickup. "Wanna come to my cottage later?" Terry whispered to me. "I'll show you my portfolio."

"Sure, I'd love to."

Terry and I spent the rest of the night sitting side by side in the back of the pickup truck, our legs hanging off the edge. In the middle of the second movie, Terry dozed off, resting his head against the side of the truck. If our families weren't present, I would have let him lean against me with his head on my shoulder. I kept my hand between our thighs, enjoying being this close to him, wishing I could be closer.

Just so Mike wouldn't ask a million questions, I pretended to get ready for bed. Once he was asleep, I left the inn and went to Terry's cottage. "What took you so long?" Terry asked, opening his door.

"I had to wait for Mike to go to bed."

"Have a seat."

Nervously, I fidgeted with my fingers as I sat on the couch in front of the fireplace. Holding a sketchbook, Terry sat beside me. He opened it up to a black and white drawing of a naked woman. "Is she an ex-girlfriend?" I asked.

"No," he laughed. "She's an art student at the University of Vermont." He flipped to another page. Again, the same woman.

"She likes to be naked, huh?"

"I like to draw and she doesn't mind posing."

"They're very good. I could never draw like this."

"Have you ever tried?"

"No. I could never... "

"Because she's naked?"

"No, it's not that. I just don't think I'm good enough. Anyway, I don't know of any women who would do it."

"It doesn't have to be women."

Hmm... maybe he's right.

"You wanna try me?" he asked.

My cheeks burned, envisioning him lying naked on the couch.

"Come on, let's do it," he said, shedding his clothes before I answered. Once he was naked, he lay back down, dropping his feet in my lap.

"I don't think I can," I said as Terry handed me his sketchbook and pencil.

"You'll never know unless you try. Now pull up a chair and get to work."

I did as he said, sitting in a chair in front of the couch. My hand shook as I held the pencil, staring down at the blank piece of paper. "I'm afraid I won't do you justice," I said.

"Don't be so hard on yourself."

As I drew an outline of Terry's body, he attempted to ease my nerves by talking as if there was nothing strange about what we were doing. He told me all about his goals in life and his future plans. I liked listening to him.

"I want to host a camp someday here on the Lachance property, a camp for kids Mike's age. Wouldn't that be cool?" He didn't wait for me to respond before continuing. "There's a lot of underprivileged kids out there who would love to go to camp. Summer camp shouldn't just be for rich kids, so I've been thinking about getting grants and raising money to give all kids a chance."

"That's cool."

"What are your goals?"

"Hmm," I contemplated, distracted by Terry's beautiful naked body, trying to figure out how to capture it on paper. "To graduate college, have a successful career, maybe fall in love and have a family."

"That's nice, but what are *your* goals, not your parents' goals?"

No one had ever asked me that before. I had to think a minute. "I want to be happy." It seemed so simple but true.

"I hope you achieve that goal."

"Stop talking. I need to focus."

Since most of my drawings tended to be more abstract than realistic, Terry's portrait wasn't all that different from my others, except this drawing contained body parts I'd never drawn before. My body burned the whole time. By the time I finished at three in the morning, I hoped I had captured his beauty. Closing the sketchbook, I got up from the chair and sat back down beside Terry on the couch.

"Can I see it?" he asked, sitting up. He sat so close to me, his bare legs rubbed against mine. I half-nodded, letting Terry take the sketchbook from me. He glanced at me, opening the book to my first ever nude portrait.

"It's not very good," I said.

"No, it's great. You're very generous." I felt myself blush as he traced his black and white cock on the paper.

"That's what I see."

"You see things differently. You see me and not just my dick."

As our eyes met, I jumped to my feet before I did something I'd regret. I figured now was the perfect time to say goodnight.

"You don't have to go," Terry said as I headed to the door, his eyes begging me to stay.

"It's three in the morning," I reminded him. "You have to get up in a few hours. I'll see you tomorrow."

I sprinted back to the inn, my body on fire, desperate for some kind of sexual release. I found that release over the toilet.

7

Chapter 7

The Lachances hosted a dance every Saturday night, and this Saturday night we celebrated Thomas Prescott and Frankie Lachance's fiftieth birthdays. Like a proper ball, women dressed up in fancy gowns and makeup, and men wore suits, except me. This was my summer vacation; there was no way I was dressing up. After an hour of pleading and begging, my mother talked Mike and I into wearing a tie. My thoughts turned to Terry, imagining him in a suit or tux, his hair tucked behind his ears. I bet he'd look great in a suit or tux.

When we showed up, I found Terry working hard, wearing an apron, dungarees, and work boots. For five minutes, he stopped running around so he could lead the group in an acoustic rendition of *Happy Birthday*.

So far, I considered this summer the best summer of my life. Terry made me feel good about myself. He made me believe I could do anything as long as I tried. He was the reason I got up at the butt crack of dawn. Just thinking about him put more than a smile on my face. I was so incredibly attracted to him, I'd lay awake at night, jerking off, hoping I wouldn't wake Mike.

"This is so lame," Mike said, working on his third piece of birthday cake while I held a beer, wondering where Terry was.

"Why don't you ask a girl to dance?" I suggested.

"No way." At twelve, Mike showed an interest in girls but still preferred climbing trees.

One girl, around thirteen or fourteen, summoned enough courage to ask me to dance, something Terry predicted the other day. I didn't want to hurt her feelings and say no, so I danced with her. I danced with another girl and another girl as if I was the only young guy there. A few years ago, my mother taught me how to dance before my cousin's wedding. She said I was "a natural." Since I liked to dance, I didn't mind dancing with these girls, although I wished they were someone else. Amid spinning a teen girl around, Terry lurked between the dining room and kitchen. As our eyes met, he smiled, waving to me.

"Excuse me," I said to the girl. "I think I need a break."

"Will you come back?" she asked with a pout.

"Maybe." Terry's eyes followed me as I approached him. "I feel like I'm at a prom for old people," I said to him.

"I saw you dancing with some girls. I'm sure they'd make lovely wives in ten years' time."

I shrugged, rolling my eyes.

"You're a good dancer," he said. "I have two left feet. I tried dancing once, my freshman year of high school. It didn't go well."

"Come with me." I grabbed his apron, leading him to the back of the inn. "I'll show you."

"Show me what?"

"How to dance." Desperate to get close to him and willing to do anything, a dance lesson seemed harmless, maybe even acceptable. "I'll show you it's not so hard."

"I don't think I can do this. I'm working."

"You can take a break for five minutes." My hand trembled as I took Terry's hand in mine. I guided his other hand to my shoulder. As a classic waltz played inside, I centered my hand in the middle of his back. "Just count," I instructed him. "One, two, three… " Our eyes remained fixed, laughing each time he stepped on my foot. "Ow," I said jokingly.

More relaxed and confident by the third song, I spun him around, showing off some moves. I pulled him closer to me, so close our chests touched, his cheek against mine. My heart beat out of my chest, sweat trickling down the sides of my face. As our dancing slowed, I pulled away from him, our faces mere inches apart. From that point on, I had no control over my actions. My clammy hand landed on the back of his neck, and I did the unthinkable: I kissed him.

And I kissed him on his mouth, acting on my feelings for the first time in my life. After that brief, humiliating, yet exhilarating, kiss, Terry stared back at me, as stunned as I was at my indiscretion. My lips tingled, my heart raced, longing to kiss him again. "God, I'm sorry," I gasped. "I'm so sorry."

Terry stood there, silent and expressionless. He was probably contemplating punching this disgusting, perverted asshole in the face. Embarrassed and ashamed, I ran off. I'd never forgive myself for acting on my impulses. My summer was over, and I planned on begging my parents to take me home in the morning.

Storming into my room, I slammed my door, locking it so Mike wouldn't bother me. In a huff, I stripped down to my underwear and threw myself into bed. Curled up under the covers, I sniffed back my boyish, shameful tears, annoyed by the knock on the door. "Go away!" I shouted, my voice muffled by the blankets over my head.

"Scott, it's me," Terry said, his voice quiet and calm. "Can I come in?"

My body froze. I didn't know what to say or do. What if he planned on telling my parents I was both sick and perverted?

"I know you're in there. I'm coming in." Even though I had locked my door, Terry used his key to open it. As he entered my room, I rolled over, turning my back to him. My breathing grew shallower as Terry approached the bed. "Look at me, Scott." He placed a hand on my shoulder. "Come on, turn around. You shouldn't have run off. You didn't wait for me to respond."

"What are you talking about?" I sat up. "What do you mean *respond*? You were going to hit me, right? Because I'm so disgusting and weird."

"Shut up." He sat on my bed. "Are you blind or what?" He wiped away my tears with his hand and kissed my cheek. Relieved, I threw my arms around him, hugging him tightly. I inhaled against his neck, breathing in his scent. "I'm crazy about you," he said in my ear. "I didn't know what to do, either. At the lake... "

And I thought he was fast asleep. "Why didn't you say anything?" I pulled away from him.

"The same reason you didn't. I wanted to kiss you for a long time."

"A long time? We've only known each other for a week."

"I feel like I've known you forever. I really want to kiss you. Can I kiss you?"

I nodded. With his other hand, he held the side of my face, bringing his lips to mine. Electric sparks ran through my body, something I'd never experienced with any girl. The more we kissed, the more my body burned. I pushed the blankets to the floor, kissing Terry harder. Just as our tongues made contact, he broke away from me, his hand now on my bare waist.

"The only girl I ever kissed was Elizabeth Carlson in the eighth grade, and I only kissed her because kids dared me to kiss her," he said.

"You've never kissed anyone else?" I asked, my fingers still in his hair.

Ashamed, he shook his head, looking down and away.

"So you have nothing to compare me to."

"If I did, I bet there'd be no comparison."

"There is no comparison." I squeezed his shoulder. I had kissed many girls but no kiss ever felt like Terry's kisses. My lips grazed over his forehead as his fingers pinched my waist. Terry lifted his head, pairing his lips with mine. We resumed where we left off, his tongue in my mouth and mine in his, my excitement noticeable through my underwear. Terry smiled against my lips as I held my hand over it. "Sorry."

"I'm flattered." He traced my collarbone with his finger. "Did you think I didn't notice your killer hard-on the other day? Maybe you can show me how Mary Ellen did it."

"Yeah, okay." Desperate, and maybe a little too eager, I pushed down the front of my underwear. Terry burst into laughter, kissing my mouth. "Come on, get in bed with me." The pounding on the door put an end to everything.

"Scottie, open up!" Mike yelled behind the locked door.

"Shit," I muttered as Terry broke away from me, throwing the blanket over my half-naked body.

"Scottie, come on! I wanna go to bed," Mike whined.

"It's okay," Terry said, standing up. "We'll see each other tomorrow."

"Terry, is that you in there?" Mike asked.

As Terry opened the door, we found Mike standing there with his arms folded across his chest, irritated we locked him out. "What were you guys doing in there? You look weird."

"It's hot in here," Terry said.

"Yeah, I guess you're right," Mike said, walking into the room. "Can we go water skiing tomorrow?"

"Sure," Terry replied. "I'll see you guys tomorrow." Terry glanced over his shoulder once before leaving.

As Mike was about to say something, I flung off the blankets and ran to the bathroom, quickly pushing down my underwear. My cock throbbed in my hand, envisioning Terry naked and swinging from the rope by the lake. It took all of thirty seconds to finish, a world record for me. Satisfied and content, I returned to my bed, wondering what tomorrow would bring. I couldn't wait to find out.

8

Chapter 8

Terry

The day after Scott's arrival, the day he hid in his room, sulking and listening to the Red Sox, I knew he'd be a challenge. I always liked a challenge. My goal with Scott was to break that protective shell of his, freeing himself to have fun. He proved easy to break.

The way he looked at me, the way he licked the salt off the palm of my hand, and the way he undressed me with his eyes gave off so many obvious signals that pointed to one thing: he wanted more than a friendship.

And so did I.

Within a very short time, we formed a close bond, so close I trusted him more than I had ever trusted anyone else. I trusted him enough to share my secret place with him, the only person — other than my dad — who knew about it. Scott also looked great naked, definitely an athlete, albeit "a mediocre one," or so he said.

Girls never interested me. At fourteen, a group of kids teased me and bullied me into kissing Elizabeth Carlson, the overweight, pimple-faced outcast of the school. Succumbing to peer pressure, I kissed her in the hallway after lunch. I didn't have the heart to break the news to her that I only kissed her because of a dare. Although we never kissed again, I strung her along until the end of the school year, pretending I liked her.

For a long time, I thought I'd never have romantic feelings for anyone, but in high school I realized I was wrong. Rather, I discovered I had lots of feelings for half the high school football team. Yeah, I was one of those guys.

As I filled a pot with fresh waffle batter at six in the morning, Scott sat alone at a table in the empty restaurant. Not much of a morning person, Mike often dragged Scott out of bed until he and I developed this closer-than-average friendship. After completing my task, I grabbed a pot of coffee and two mugs and greeted him. All I wanted to do was throw myself at him and resume where we left off last night. "Good morning," I said, pouring him a cup of coffee. "What are you doing up so early? I have to work."

"I like to watch you work." He blushed. "And I have nothing better to do." Scott stood up and kissed my lips as if he'd been waiting to do that all night.

"You shouldn't do that," I warned him. "There's people in the kitchen and guests will show up any minute."

He rolled his eyes, sitting back down in his chair, folding his arms across his chest. Whenever he didn't get his way, or when he was told off, he'd roll his eyes and sulk. He was so damn cute. "Are you busy later?" he asked.

"Yeah, I'm taking you and Mikey water skiing." I couldn't wait to see him up on water skis, to see him in one of his tight-fitting swimsuits again.

"Maybe after lunch you could give me another rowing lesson."

"Sure." I smiled. "I'd love to. Well, I better get back to work. I'll see you later."

"See you later." He smiled, squeezing my hand.

"Good morning, boys," my dad said brightly, appearing out of nowhere. My mother always said he had "quiet feet," notorious for sneaking up on people. Scott pulled his hand away just in time.

"Hi, Dad," I said. "I'm just... well, I'm going back to work. Just poured Scott some coffee."

"Why don't you take some time off and have breakfast with Scott outside," my dad suggested. "It's a beautiful morning... nice and quiet on the lake. No one's out there right now. Sometimes it's the best time of day."

"Yeah, let's go," Scott said, already heading to the breakfast bar. We loaded up two plates with toast and scrambled eggs and sat behind a tree by the bank of the lake. The lake was quiet, not a soul around at six thirty in the morning.

As his eyes met mine, I caressed his scratchy cheek with my fingers, neither of us interested in eating breakfast. Although he took a shower, he didn't shave. I liked him a little disheveled and unshaven. After scanning the area to make sure we were alone, I kissed his lips once. He immediately kissed me back with one long, lingering kiss.

As we kissed, Scott pulled me into his lap. He reached under my t-shirt, sucking my bottom lip. I didn't resist as he lifted my shirt over my head, followed by his own shirt. Our bare chests pressed together, my legs hooked behind his back, our lips locked. I was so turned on, my shorts grew uncomfortably tight. "What are you doing?" I asked, shocked that Scott had the balls to whip out his dick in a public area.

"No one's here," he whispered, his hand wrapped around his growing erection.

"Then why are you whispering?"

"Shut up." He kissed me.

Although he'd seen mine before, I didn't have the guts to do it, not out here. But Scott didn't stop, quietly jerking off. I kissed him harder as he moaned into my mouth, releasing himself on my stomach. Once he finished, his body fell limp in my arms, panting. I looked down, discovering Scott had made a mess of both my stomach and shorts.

"Oops," Scott laughed, attempting to clean off the residue with his hand. Instead, he smeared it while pressing his other hand on my crotch. He continued to massage my cock through my shorts until my body shuddered. Scott kissed my mouth before I cried out. "I can't believe you just came in your shorts."

"You're so crazy," I laughed against his lips.

As one family emerged, I jumped out of Scott's lap and ran into the water. Scott barely had enough time to zip up. Laughing, he followed me into the water and jumped on my back. If I was strong enough, I would have flipped him over my head. He kissed my cheek and hopped off my back before swimming to the dock.

Lying side by side, we basked in the early morning sun. Since I didn't get much sleep last night, I dozed off. Like my dad said, morning was often the best time of day out here. It was even better with Scott Prescott lying beside me.

"Wake up!" a familiar voice shouted.

With one eye open, I observed Scott's baby brother hovering over him, holding a bucket of water. Scott continued to sleep despite Mike's boisterous voice. I laughed to myself, waiting for him to dump the bucket over his head. "Okay, here it goes," Mike warned. As he poured the water, Scott bolted upright, rubbing the water out of his eyes.

"You're so dead," Scott said.

Mike tossed the bucket at me and jumped off the dock, swimming as if his life depended on it. Scott dove in after him, quickly catching up to him. He dunked him under water and held him there as he flailed. Sometimes I wished I had an annoying baby brother.

* * *

At fifty years old, my dad was still a pro at water skiing. He even showed Mike and Scott the proper techniques. It was always best to start off with one ski; two skis were more difficult to maneuver.

For half an hour, Mike tried to get up and failed each time, becoming more and more irate. Scott's roaring laughter fueled Mike's anger. If I hadn't been at the wheel of the boat, I would have elbowed Scott and told him to knock it off. "I hope you fall flat on your face," I said to him as he laughed.

But Scott didn't fall flat on his face. He got up on the first try, infuriating Mike.

"He's older," my dad said to Mike, now at the wheel, attempting to calm him down. "His arms and legs are stronger than yours." And Scott had very nice arms and legs, far more muscular than mine.

"You can always try again tomorrow," I said, my eyes focused on Scott, admiring his athletic frame.

Back in the boat, with my dad at the wheel, Scott bounced his damp knee against mine. His flirtatious grin told me he was doing it on purpose.

"Aren't you going?" Mike asked me.

"Get out there," my dad urged me.

"I'm going, I'm going." Even though I'd been water skiing since I was five years old, it always took me at least three tries to get up. Distracted by Scott's eyes on me, I struggled today. After the seventh try, I was up and going strong until the two brothers played a trick on me. They pushed down their swimsuits, exposing their pale bare asses, mooning me. As I landed face-first in the water, the boys rolled over laughing in the boat.

Scott was going to pay for that.

9

Chapter 9

Scott

Mike had some good ideas from time to time and mooning Terry was one of them. Curious to see his reaction, I didn't hesitate when Mike whispered his idea to me. Mike and I both roared with laughter as Terry fell flat on his face.

"Get off me," Terry said as I attempted to pull him back into the boat. "I should kick both your asses."

Mike and I laughed so hard we cried. Even Terry's dad laughed, but Terry wasn't in the mood for laughing. He chose not to sit next to me.

"I could have gotten killed, you know that?" Terry lectured us, then directed his attention to me. While sitting across from me, he half-smiled. Sulking and pouting weren't in his nature. "You're going to get it, you know that?"

"Ooo, what am I going to get?" I said.

"I have to think about it."

Despite the dark, ominous clouds, Terry and I went for our typical afternoon boat ride. He sat behind me, guiding my arms as I attempted to row. He rested his chin on my shoulder, his lips occasionally brushing against my neck, easily distracting me. I almost lost the oars again, a daily occurrence.

We both stripped naked and took turns swinging from the rope. Every time I tried to get close to him, he swam away, teasing me by playing hard to get. I couldn't wait to kiss him again, to feel his naked body against mine, to do other things to him. He suddenly walked out of the lake, leaving me baffled and confused.

"Terry," I called to him, but he ignored me, heading to the trees, like he planned on taking a walk barefoot and naked through the woods. When he didn't respond, I bolted out of the water, tackling him to the ground. "Stop playing hard to get," I said, yanking his hair back. "I know you want me as much as I want you."

"Thanks a lot, Scottie. Now I'm covered in mud."

"Don't call me Scottie," I said through clenched teeth.

"Okay, whatever you say, Scottie."

I playfully bit his neck.

"Hey, do that again," he laughed. "Come on, Scottie, do it."

Instead of biting him with my teeth, my lips clamped down on his neck, sucking hard. As I sucked, my cock hardened against his ass.

"Oh, my God," Terry whispered. "Is that you?"

Letting go of his hair, I scooted down his body, planting kisses all along his spine, landing at his tailbone. He inhaled, gasping as I kissed each butt cheek. Both aroused and nervous, Terry's body tensed.

"Now roll over and let me see you," I said. "Roll over or I'll tickle you to death."

"What if I like to be tickled?"

I dug my fingers into his sides, causing him to wiggle and squirm, laughing hysterically.

"Truce!" he yelled in a fit of giggles. With some hesitation, he finally rolled over. Blades of grass speckled his body, with mud splattered in various parts and crevices. I scooped up a handful of mud and smeared it over his pretty face. "Asshole," he laughed, flinging a handful of mud at me.

We rolled around in the grass and mud, fighting and wrestling with each other. Terry, out of breath, escaped, running into the water with me right behind him.

"You're not getting away from me again," I said, pulling him to me. Our laughter dwindled as I hugged him, sliding my hands down his back and over his ass. I squeezed both cheeks, eliciting a sigh from him. With my hands firmly on his ass, I pushed him closer to me, pressing my naked body against his. My finger ran up and down his crack, wondering what it would be like to be inside him. Would it hurt? Yeah, it probably would.

Terry wrapped his legs around me, allowing me to carry him out of the water. I lay on top of him, rubbing my cock against his while his hands roamed down my backside. I broke away from him, bringing my lips to his chest. He combed his fingers through my hair, sighing as I kissed his stomach, making my way farther down. His eyes peered down at me as I dragged my tongue up and down each side of his pelvis.

As he gazed up into the sky, I kissed the base of his cock. Relaxed, his legs flopped to either side of him, allowing me full access. His chest heaved in and out, my tongue teasing him, circling his shaft. And then I went for it. Terry's back arched as I took him in my mouth, little by little. I remembered the first time I received my first blow job. I only lasted thirty seconds, too, just like Terry.

"Oh, fuck," he muttered, releasing himself in my mouth. "Oh, fuck, Scott. I'm sorry. Shit, I'm dizzy."

I scooted back up his body and kissed his mouth.

"Let me do you," he said.

"It's too late." While performing my first blow job, I jerked off, but Terry was too busy enjoying himself to notice. "But there'll be other times."

Terry held my face in his hands, his eyes more serious than I'd seen them all day. "What's going to happen to us?" he asked.

"Nothing. No one has to know about us." If my ultra conservative parents ever found out about me and Terry's relationship, they'd disown me, and my dad would end his lifelong friendship with Frankie. My parents would never accept a gay son.

"How could something be wrong when it feels so right?" Terry said.

"It doesn't feel wrong to me, either. Let's go for another swim."

During our final swim before heading back, Terry left me stranded in the water. One minute he was swimming circles around me, the next minute he was gone, running out of the water yet again. "Hey! Where are you going?"

As I tread water, I observed Terry pick up my swimsuit with that same mischievous grin I saw earlier. He turned to face me, swinging it around and around. "Don't you even think about it," I said, my heart beating nervously, afraid of what he was about to do.

"I told you I'd get you for what you did to me."

As I approached him, Terry backed up, getting closer and closer to the trees. Just as I was about to reach him, he flung my swimsuit high up into the air, so high it landed on a tree limb far above our heads. There was no way of reaching it without a ladder. "Oops," Terry said. "I didn't mean to throw it that hard."

"That's great." Fuming, I shoved him. "Now what am I going to do? I can't walk around naked."

"Why not? You look good naked."

I gave him the middle finger and stormed off. As I sat in the boat with my knees to my chest, I watched Terry unsuccessfully try to retrieve my swimsuit with a stick. If I had brought a towel, I wouldn't have been in this predicament. "Get me the hell out of here," I said.

On the ride back, I refused to look at him, too pissed off. He didn't deserve the blow job I just gave him, the first one I'd ever given. I hated him and briefly wished I'd never met him.

"Did you swallow?" he asked, rowing.

Although tempted to laugh, I didn't, determined to stay pissed off. Yes, I swallowed, but he didn't give me much of a choice. If he wasn't such a jerk, I'd let him do it again. "Shut up. Don't talk to me ever again."

"It was an accident. I didn't mean to do it."

"You're an asshole," I said, continuing to sulk until we reached land. "That's the one and only blow job I'll ever give you."

"You're unbelievable," Terry said in exasperation. He didn't say another word, not even as he docked the boat.

"Hey," I said as he stepped out of the boat. "You're going to get me a towel, right?"

He walked away, completely ignoring me. The asshole abandoned me in the boat. I cupped myself in my hands and sprinted across the grounds and into the inn. I'd never run so fast in my entire life. Because of the pending storm, few people were around to see this naked spectacle.

My room was empty, so I didn't have to explain myself to Mike. I took a marathon long shower. If I wasn't starving, I would have stayed in my room all night, stewing in anger.

By the time I reached the restaurant, every table was full. My family, along with Susan and Frankie Lachance, sat at a table by the window overlooking the lake. Scumbag Terry was noticeably missing. Outside, thunder rumbled, rain pounding the windows and roof of the restaurant.

"So nice of you to join us," my mother said in that passive-aggressive way of hers.

"Terry's taking a nap," Susan said as if to read my mind. "He's playing in the pub tonight. We're expecting a large crowd because of the rain."

Envisioning Terry's infectious smile, I contemplated going to the pub to see him perform. What could I say? He was cute and owed me a favor. I certainly didn't want to go to the movies with Mike and my parents.

On this dreary night, the Lachance pub overflowed with people, more than usual. In the corner, Terry sat on a stool, playing and singing his favorite Simon and Garfunkel song, *The Boxer.* As I hopped on a bar stool, Terry smiled at me. I didn't smile back, not until *The Boxer* ended and a new song started. I couldn't help but smile as he played *Blackbird.* After finishing, Terry put down his guitar and headed to me. The bartender placed two beers in front of me even before he said anything.

"Forgive me?" Terry said as I leaned against the bar. He pushed my knees apart and stood between them, sipping his beer. "I guess I owe you a swimsuit."

"Yeah, you owe me." The man sitting beside me walked off, allowing Terry to take his place. Terry spent more time at the bar than in the corner singing and playing, the incident at the lake long forgotten. Music played from the 1950s-style jukebox.

Just after eleven thirty, the last couple left the pub. I helped Terry and the bartender wash down the tables and sweep the floor. When the bartender left, Terry and I weren't ready to say goodnight. He selected a song from the jukebox, a song I immediately recognized, a classic I'd often hear at home. The smooth, jazzy voice of Ella Fitzgerald sang *Dream a Little Dream of Me.* My parents preferred listening to music than watching TV, so Mike and I grew up listening to Ella Fitzgerald, Billie Holiday, and Duke Ellington, in addition to rock-and-roll classics like Elvis and The Everly Brothers. Terry reached for my hand and pulled me to my feet.

"You want to dance right here?" I asked.

"Yes," Terry said. "No one's here. Come on, you're a great dancer."

Terry placed his hand on my shoulder while I positioned my hand on his lower back. I held him close to me, taking the lead. Throughout the next three songs, he only stepped on my foot twice. I could have danced with him all night and let him step on my foot a million times.

10

Chapter 10

Terry

Through the torrential rain, Scott held my hand, pulling me along as we ran from the pub to my cottage. Drenched to the bone, we peeled our wet clothes off our bodies, leaving them in a heap on the floor.

In case I ever had the urge—or need— to start a fire, I had stacked logs and twigs beside the fireplace. I always hoped to share a romantic fire with someone someday. While Scott stood there shivering and naked, I gathered up some towels from the bathroom. In the middle of drying off, Scott kissed me, continuing to shiver.

"I'll start a fire," I said, backing away from him. "You're freezing." I wrapped a blanket around my body and knelt on the floor in front of the fireplace. As I chucked some logs in, Scott dropped his damp towel on top of my head. He got under the blanket with me.

So many things drew me to Scott. He had these amazing brown eyes with freckles on the bridge of his nose that matched the ones on his shoulders. Most importantly, we made each other laugh, and laughter and humor were important to me. Besides, we had this incredible, intense attraction to each other and an unusual bond I had never shared with anyone before.

His hand crept up my thigh, aiming for my groin. Unable to control myself, I threw myself at him, pinning him underneath me, my backside exposed but warmed by the roaring fire. He raked his fingers through my hair as my lips trailed down his body.

My hand trembled as I held his cock, the first time I ever touched it. He looked down at me with wide eyes, waiting with bated breath. I playfully bounced his cock against my tongue. He was fun to tease. Impatient, he opened his legs wider, grasping clumps of my hair, pushing me to him. Scott inhaled as I licked his shaft like a lollipop, culminating at the tip. I opened my mouth, allowing his cock inside it.

Although I gagged, I took more and more in, releasing him seconds later. I scattered kisses all over his neck and chest, my fingers gripping his waist, making my way back to his cock. I wanted to be inside him. I started by inserting the tip of my finger. Gasping for breath, Scott yanked my head back, crying out as his cum shot unexpectedly at me. He reached for me, his body convulsing. As he finished against my stomach, he kissed my mouth hard, sucking my bottom lip.

After regaining his composure, Scott "returned the favor," as he would say. Exhausted, our bodies gave out, and we collapsed in my bed around two in the morning. Scott fell asleep in my arms, one of his legs draped over mine.

Come morning, I found Scott sleeping on his stomach, hugging all the pillows. As my alarm clock rang at the usual time of five in the morning, I was so tired I couldn't get up. "Shut that fucking thing off," Scott grumbled, knocking the alarm clock to the floor.

An hour later, I dragged myself out of bed. Dressed and showered, I ran to the inn, embarrassed I was so late. My dad took my place, laying out the plates and silverware, getting ready to open for breakfast.

"It's the third day you're late," he said. "Today is the latest yet. What's going on?"

"Sorry. I stayed up too late again," I said, tying my apron.

"Where's Scott?" my dad interrupted my futile apologies.

"Scott?" I swallowed hard. "I assume he's still in bed. He usually comes down around seven."

"You mean he's asleep in your bed?"

"No," I lied, but I was the worst liar in the world, especially when my parents confronted me. "Okay," I confessed. "He's asleep in my bed. We were up late. He had too much to drink again and he passed out." That was partly true, except for the "too much to drink" part. He only had two beers all night.

As I went to fill up the napkin dispenser, my dad grabbed my arm firmer than usual. "Look, son, I like Scott. He's a good kid, but I know Tommy." He referred to Scott's father. "And I don't know what he'll do if he ever found out— "

"There's nothing to find out," I cut him off. "We're friends."

"No," my dad said. "Tommy and I are friends. You and Scott are more than friends."

As a quiet and obedient child, I was never one to get in trouble or be disrespectful. My parents never had a reason to tell me off or ground me. For one of the first times in my life, I had to defend myself. "Have you ever met anyone who could see into your soul?" I asked.

"Yes," my dad replied. "As a matter of fact, I married her."

Before continuing my job, I paused, swallowing my tears because I could never marry whom I wanted to marry or have what my parents had. "Drop it, okay?" I said. "Let me get back to work."

"I just worry about you, that's all."

"Well, don't. I've never given you reason to worry, so don't start now."

"I'm your father. I'll never stop worrying. Be careful, Terry. I'd hate to see you get hurt." There was nothing to worry about. Scott would never hurt me. He could never hurt anyone.

Around eight, I spotted Scott with his family, bored, his elbow propped on the table. He often had that bored look on his face whenever he was with his family, most often in the morning. He wasn't much of a morning person. When our eyes met, his bored expression lifted, and we shared a smile. My body yearned for him all over again.

* * *

During tonight's bonfire activities, I watched Scott cook two hot dogs on a stick, his brother not too far away. Mike idolized his big brother, but Scott never realized it, thinking he was nothing more than a royal pain in the ass, although he was one of those, too.

Every once in a while, Scott caught me staring at him, and he'd smile before turning his attention back to his hot dogs. As soon as he finished with his hot dogs, he moved on to the marshmallows. I loved watching him cook and eat marshmallows. I loved watching him do everything.

"Why aren't you singing tonight?" he asked, his tongue poking out the side of his mouth, concentrating as he stuck marshmallows on his stick.

"I'm not in the mood," I said. All I wanted to do was get Scott back to my cottage. He was so irresistible I couldn't help myself, eager to touch him. Purposely bumping into him, I tried to be discreet as I ran my hand down his arm. His body tensed at my touch, making me want him even more. Scott shoved his roasted marshmallow in my face, making my face a sticky, gooey mess. He laughed at his little stunt, proceeding to roast another marshmallow.

"I wanna lick it off," Scott whispered. "I wanna lick it all off."

My cheeks burned, my face flushed, imagining Scott's tongue over my lips and chin. I looked forward to it. The darkness hid my face so Scott's dad couldn't see it as he stood beside us. His mother was busy socializing with other guests, bragging about something or other, whether it was the success of her husband's business, her social status in the community, or Scott's acceptance into Rochester Tech. She had every reason to be proud, but she had a habit of going on and on.

"Beautiful night, huh?" Tom Prescott said. "I think I'll miss this place, but I'll be back in a few weeks and then Scottie will be off to college. I assume you're heading off, too?" he said to me.

"Uh... yeah... Labor Day weekend."

"I don't want to talk about college," Scott said.

"Scottie's a little nervous," Mr. Prescott said. "That's to be expected, though. Scottie's never done well with change. He hates doing anything that's different."

"Dad... " Scott warned as if he was about to blow his top or storm off in a temper tantrum. I'd seen him do that before. "Stop talking about it."

"Okay, okay, I'll stop. I'm heading in, anyway."

"Good," Scott mumbled under his breath. In frustration, Scott tossed his stick into the fire.

"Don't be a baby," I said as his dad walked away. "Come back to my place."

"What are you guys talking about?" Mike butted in.

"Nothing," Scott said. "I'm going to hang out at Terry's for a little while."

"Can I come?" he asked.

"No," Scott said. "It's after ten o'clock. Go to bed."

"It's summer vacation. I can stay up as late as I want."

"No, you can't. I'm telling Mom."

Mike chased after him as he approached their mother. She nodded in my direction, waving to me, giving Scott the okay to come back with me. His parents were overprotective, always wanting to know his whereabouts.

"Come on," Scott said to me, tugging at my arm. "Let's go."

Just as my door closed, Scott pushed me against it, kissing me hard on my mouth. He stuck out his tongue, dragging it over my cheek, licking off the dried, roasted marshmallow on my face, his tongue making its way to my upper lip. He lifted my shirt over my head and brought his tongue to my collarbone. His tongue slithered down the center of my chest. He got down on his knees, planting kisses all along my stomach and waist while undoing my shorts.

"Scott," I whispered to him as he pushed back my cock, kissing my balls. "God, that feels good."

Cradling my balls in his hand, he sucked my cock until it was good and hard. I would have let him continue, but I had other things in mind. As we kissed, I backed Scott onto my bed and yanked his shorts and underwear off with one hard tug. We moaned into each other's mouths as he opened his legs, hooking them around my thighs, trying to get closer. His legs loosened as I broke away from him to kiss his chest. He guided my head down his body to the area where he wanted it.

He sighed happily as my tongue swirled around his cock, toying and teasing him just the way he liked it. As I licked the tip, he played with my hair, twirling strands around his fingers. His back arched slightly as I opened my mouth, taking him in it. He watched me intently as my head bobbed up and down, his cock slipping between my lips.

"Roll over," I instructed him.

He swallowed hard, half-smiling, before following my instructions.

"Don't be scared," I said, although I was nervous as hell. Scott clutched the pillow. "Don't be nervous," I told him, running my finger up and down his crack. The bartender, George, pulled me aside the other day, and gave me some advice. He also gave me a bottle and told me I may "need it." Now was the time when I needed it. I squeezed the clear liquid on my finger and circled Scott's entrance with it. He inhaled as I pushed my finger in him. As I withdrew, he exhaled, moaning as I reinserted it, urging me to continue. He was ready, but was I? I propped him up on his hands and knees, and rubbed my cock against him. Scott moaned into the pillow as I inched inside him. He was tight, closing in around me, my cock throbbing inside him. "Tell me to stop and I'll stop," I said in his ear.

"Don't stop."

Scott's body relaxed and his moans grew louder, not the sounds of someone in pain. He turned his head just enough to pair his lips with mine. As I thrust back and forth, gaining more and more momentum, I abruptly came inside him. He followed shortly after, crying out, his body trembling. As he breathed into the pillow, I reached for his hands, collapsing on top of him.

11

Chapter 11

Scott

All night Terry slept soundly beside me while I barely slept a wink, full of adrenaline after the night we had together. I leaned over and kissed the top of his head, combing my fingers through the back of his tangled, scraggly hair. He didn't even stir. I thought about pinching him to wake him up so we could be together again, but I wasn't that much of an asshole. Around four in the morning, I closed my eyes and finally drifted off to sleep.

The next time I opened my eyes, the sun shone brightly through the blinds. Glancing at the clock, I realized it was ten thirty and I missed breakfast again. Damn, I was starving. In his underwear, Terry paced around the room, brushing his teeth.

"I didn't have time to take a shower or brush my teeth this morning," Terry said with a mouthful of toothpaste. "I just crawled out of bed, threw on a pair of shorts and t-shirt and went to work. Your family was looking for you, too. I told them you fell asleep on the couch. I brought you some breakfast."

"Thanks. Will you come back to bed?"

"Don't you want to say goodbye to your dad? He's leaving soon. Have breakfast, then say goodbye. I'll wait for you."

"You'll wait for me in your underwear?" I got out of bed to eat the breakfast Terry laid out on the table. Naked, I sat down.

"If you want me to," he said with a flirtatious grin.

"Or maybe without them?"

Smiling with a toothbrush in his mouth, he finished up in the bathroom while I devoured my cold waffles and sausages. A few seconds later, Terry sat down beside me, placing a hand on my bare knee. "There's a great trail a few miles from here. Maybe we could go for a hike. Just the two of us." He kissed the side of my head as I bit down on a piece of sausage. His lips moved from my face to my neck, his hand sliding up my thigh.

"Yeah, sure, " I said, becoming more and more light-headed as my body reacted to Terry's lips. "Ugh. I have to say goodbye to my dad. If I don't, he'll be pissed and come looking for me and then he might find us... " My voice trailed off as Terry kissed the corner of my mouth, his hand brushing over my cock. "Terry," I warned him, but not so convincingly. "You're making me hard."

"Yeah, so I noticed." He ran a finger up my shaft.

As my cock hardened in his hand, my lips made it to Terry's. He giggled as my tongue played with his, his hand wrapped firmly around my cock, his thumb rubbing over the tip. "You're gonna make me come."

"That's the idea," he smiled against my lips. He bent down and licked the tip.

"Oh, fuck," I gasped as he took my cock in his mouth. He looked up at me and that was it. Terry held me there, letting me finish. Once he sat up, I kissed him once and hugged him. "I guess I'll go say goodbye to my dad."

The bulge in Terry's underwear was impossible not to notice, but I didn't have time to return the favor. "Don't worry about that," Terry said, placing his hands on his lap, attempting to cover himself. "I'll take care of it."

Terry continued to sit there at the table as I got dressed, his eyes on me the entire time. As I was about to open the door, I decided I had another ten minutes to spare and charged toward him.

"What are you doing?" he laughed as I pulled him to his feet. I backed him onto his bed and quickly tugged down the front of his underwear. "Wait, Scott. You don't have to. " But it was too late; his cock was already in my mouth. "Oh, my God, that's nice."

Seconds after releasing him, he came suddenly against my chin. "Oops," he laughed. "God, I'm sorry." Terry held my face, pulling me up to him. He kissed my lips once, then dragged his tongue over my chin, licking me clean. "You better go. We can catch up later."

At almost noon, my dad was ready to leave, waiting at the Prescott station wagon, irritated that no one had seen me all morning. "Where the hell have you been?"

"Hanging out," I said with a shrug.

"He was at Terry's," Mike said. "He was there all night."

"Shut up, Mike," I said. "I fell asleep on his couch."

"Why don't you take it easy on the booze, huh?" My dad assumed I passed out drunk again.

Frank's eyes drifted in my direction, making me think he suspected I didn't pass out on Terry's couch. My dad would kill me if he found out I was sleeping with Terry right under his nose.

"Be good, but have fun," my dad said to me. "I'll be back in a couple of weeks."

My dad and Frank shook hands while Susan gave him a giant hug. My dad wasn't even out of the gravel parking lot when Mike ran off to play with his new friends.

Before going back to Terry's, I brushed my teeth and took a shower. As the warm water beat down on me, I couldn't stop smiling. Preoccupied with Terry, I considered going to the University of Vermont instead of Rochester Tech. But the more I thought about it, the more I realized there was no way in hell my parents would ever let that happen. In only a month, I fell in love with a man, a love I'd never find again, and I couldn't tell anyone about it.

"What took you so long?" Terry said from his bed, sitting cross-legged and naked, holding a book. "I was getting bored."

As I stood in front of his bed, he leaned into me, breathing into my neck. "Mmm... you smell nice." He kissed my neck, undoing my shorts. "We'll go hiking later."

"You make me feel so good," I said as he pushed my shorts down. "I don't think anyone will make me feel this good again."

"Stop being so negative. Let's focus on the here and now. Not tomorrow, next month, or next year. Now."

As I stepped out of my shorts and underwear, he lifted my shirt over my head. "You look great naked," he said, sliding his hand down my chest and stomach. He ran his fingers through the dark hair surrounding my cock.

With his hands on my waist, he pulled me into bed with him. I hoped it was my turn. On top of Terry, he opened his legs, inviting and welcoming me inside him. It wasn't as easy as Terry made it seem last night. He was a virgin, too, but he didn't have any problem.

"Ow," was Terry's first word. After Terry's fifth "Ow," I gave up, kneeling upright while he laughed. I had never felt so incompetent.

"It's not funny," I said, sulking, too embarrassed and annoyed to laugh.

"Learn to laugh at yourself. Lay back."

"No, I can't do it."

"Yes, you can." He pushed me on my back and lathered something on my dick, something wet and slippery. He mounted me, rubbing my cock against his entrance and pushed down on it. The way he winced, I thought I was hurting him again. "Don't," he said as I was about to push him off me. "I'm okay."

"I can't. Just do me, okay?"

"You shouldn't give up so easily," he said, getting off me.

"Just do me," I repeated, not in the mood to discuss my shortcomings. "I like the way you fuck."

He kissed me long and hard, pushing in me, showing no hesitation. I moaned into his mouth, clawing his back, my legs wrapped around his thighs. And then he said something in my ear I'd never forget. "I love you, Scott," he whispered.

12

Chapter 12

Terry

Scott pushed me away just enough to make eye contact with me, confusion and bewilderment strewn all over his face. Not one to hide my emotions, I had no control of my mouth, and sometimes I said things I regretted. "I'm sorry. I shouldn't have said that."

"Unless you mean it. You don't seem like the type who would say something you don't mean."

Yeah, he was right about that. "It doesn't make sense, does it?" I said. "We barely know each other, yet we have this unbelievable connection."

"It doesn't have to make sense." He slid his hands all the way down my backside and over my ass. "Love is strange."

Overpowering me, he pushed me on my back, keeping me inside him. His body shuddered as he sat upright, his knees digging into my thighs. Last night Scott loved doing it this way. He kissed me hard, sucking on my bottom lip.

As he bounced up and down, I gripped his sides, my fingers digging into his skin. He held on to me, his lips clamped down on my neck. I didn't care if he left a mark. He pushed down hard on me, the two of us coming simultaneously. He buried his head in my neck, his body dead weight on top of me. The room was stifling hot, my cottage reeking of sex and sweat. Scott sat back up, steadying himself on the palms of his hands against my stomach.

"I think we both need a shower," he said. "You're all sticky." As Scott got off me, standing up, remnants of my orgasm trickled down his legs. "Oh, shit."

"Turn around. Let me see," I said flirtatiously. Embarrassed, he ran to the bathroom. "Oh, my God, that's so hot." I was turned on all over again. "Come on, let me see it. You have a great ass."

"Shut up!" he shouted behind the bathroom door. I headed to the bathroom.

"Hey, don't be like that." Without knocking, I opened the door. In the shower, Scott stood there, staring up at the shower head. "You're so cute."

"Great, I'm cute," he said, annoyed, like a moody teenager.

"There's nothing wrong with that," I said, stepping into the shower. Standing behind him, I kissed the side of his head, running my hands all the way down his backside. "Would it make you feel better if I called you handsome instead? Because you're handsome, too, and sexy as hell."

He shook his head, laughing lightly. I squeezed his butt cheeks, kissing his neck. He tilted his head down, soaking his hair before spinning around to hug me, warm water beating against his back. With his arms around me, he rested his head on my shoulder, his lips on my neck as he dragged a finger between my butt cheeks.

"I want to try again," he said.

"Later. Let's get cleaned up and get going. We can't stay here and fuck all day."

Before heading off, I raided the fridge in the restaurant, packing some snacks. I pulled out some grapes, strawberries, cheese, and two bottles of Coke. "I prefer Dr. Pepper," Scott said, looking over my shoulder. To make him happy, I grabbed a bottle of Dr. Pepper. He kissed my cheek, thanking me.

"Oh, there you are," my mother said, entering the kitchen, catching us by surprise. "I hardly see you lately. Hello there, Scott."

"Hi," Scott said, avoiding her eyes.

"I'm going hiking with Scott," I said. "I'll be back in time for the bonfire."

As I led Scott out of the kitchen, my mother stopped me. She couldn't ignore the fact that she saw Scott kiss my cheek. "Go on, Scott," my mother said. "Terry'll be there in a minute."

Scott had that worried look on his face. Nodding, I urged him to leave while reassuring him that everything was okay. I had a feeling this was going to be another conversation like the one my dad had with me.

"What are you doing?" she asked me.

"I'm going on a hike with Scott."

"What have we told you about getting involved with guests?"

"Yeah, and I've never been involved with anyone. Besides, Scott's not a guest."

"Yes, he is, and you know it."

"I can't help it. I like him, okay?" I paused for a second. "No, I love him."

"Oh boy, that's what I was afraid of. Terry, you know it can't last. Tom Prescott would never allow it, and Scott... well... he's not strong enough to sustain a homosexual relationship." Something about those last two words struck a nerve. I didn't want to believe she was right. "You're both going to get hurt."

"I won't let that happen."

"Oh, Terry," my mother sighed. "What are we going to do with you? You have such a big heart. You have to be careful. Most people aren't as progressive as we are."

Progressive... that was one of my mother's favorite words.

"And Nancy?" my mother shuddered. She and my mother barely said a word to each other, mostly because my mother didn't want to get involved in her "one upmanship," she said. Apparently, my mother was not the same caliber as she, meaning my mother was beneath her in terms of social status and class, things that were clearly important to Nancy. My mother never cared about social status or class. "I can only imagine what she'd do if she found out you were romantically involved with her golden boy. I'm getting really tired of hearing her brag about Scott's grades, batting average, and Rochester Tech."

"Scott's nothing like his parents," I said. "I gotta go. See you later." As I left the kitchen with a backpack full of snacks, I found Scott outside the inn, pacing and biting his fingernails. "Let's get out of here."

Distracted, Scott trailed behind me as I led him off the Lachance property.

"What's the matter? Can't keep up?" I teased him.

Scott didn't reply, focused on the ground as we walked toward one of my most favorite trails. "Um... Terry... do you tell your parents everything?" he asked.

I told my parents a lot of things but not everything. "No," I answered. "Do you?"

"I don't tell my parents shit. Your parents know about us, don't they?"

I hesitated before responding. "Yes, but it's not because I told them. My parents know me too well. They'd see right through me if I tried to deny it. Don't worry, they would never tell your parents. They're both afraid of what they'd do. No offense, but your dad doesn't seem like such a nice guy."

"I heard what your mother said," Scott said. "She doesn't think I'm strong enough for you."

"That's not what she said." I stopped walking, turning around to face him. "She said she doesn't think you're strong enough for this type of relationship. You know, a gay one. And, to tell you the truth, I don't know if I am, either."

"Then why are we here? We should just stop seeing each other and end it. Let's just end it right now. I'm outta here." Throwing his arms up in the air, he stormed off.

I had no intention of ruining our afternoon together, so I ran after him, hoping to make it up to him. We still had another month together, and I planned on making the most of it. I wasn't ready for this relationship to end. "Wait, Scott. Don't go. I don't want it to end. What we have... it's real. Nothing like this has ever happened to me before." As I grabbed his wrist, he came to a halt.

"Let go of me," he said, staring down at the ground.

"Look at me, Scott." As he slowly lifted up his chin, his brown eyes met mine, his cheeks streaked with tears. "I'm sorry," I said, wiping away his tears with my fingertips. "Just forget what my mother and I said. I'm more afraid of losing you than anything else."

"So, come September, we just become pen pals, is that it?" His voice quivered.

"I don't know what the answer is. All I know is that it's a beautiful day and I'm going for a hike. You can go back if you want, but I'd rather you come with me."

I backed away from him and resumed walking. Scott caught up to me, slipping his hand in mine. We stopped at a clearing that overlooked the magnificent green mountains of Vermont. I dug out a blanket from my backpack and spread it out. Usually I'd spend an afternoon out here by myself reading a book, but I preferred to spend it with Scott. He brought his arm around my waist as we sat on the blanket. We ended up having a beautiful afternoon together.

13

Chapter 13

Scott

After a bright, sunny day, the rain returned with a vengeance, forcing the Lachances to cancel the bonfire. In lieu of the bonfire, my mother took Mike and I out to dinner with another family. Their father also left, leaving the mother alone with their three daughters. For a whole evening, I had to listen to two gossipy women, a twelve-year-old brat, (namely my brother) and seventeen, thirteen, and eleven-year-old girls, all talking way too much. Tabitha, Kimberly, and Raquel were their names.

Tabitha? What a name, I scoffed in my head. The names Kimberly and Raquel weren't much better. Mike and thirteen-year-old Kimberly developed a little crush on each other, judging by their pink cheeks every time one spoke. The seventeen-year-old had her eyes on me, too, blushing every time my eyes accidentally drifted in her direction. But there was only one person on my mind, and it wasn't some silly girl.

"Tabitha's pretty, isn't she?" my mother whispered to me.

"Yeah, I guess," I said indifferently, wishing my mother sat anywhere else but next to me.

"There's a dance on Saturday night. Wouldn't it be nice if you had a date?"

"Maybe I'll dance with her," I said to get my mother off my back.

For the rest of the night, I tuned everyone out, preoccupied with Terry. As soon as we got back, I went to the pub. In the corner, he sat on his usual stool, playing a song I vaguely recognized. While Mike hung out with his new friends, playing lame board games in the lobby, my mother went to bed.

In mid-song, Terry smiled at me as I sat on the last available stool at the bar. After finishing the song, he put down his guitar and came over to me. Since there was nowhere to sit, Terry squeezed between me and the person next to me. Before he said anything, the bartender poured him a beer. "Thanks, George," Terry said with his usual warm smile.

"What song was that?" I asked.

"*Words of Love*," he replied with a hand on my back. My heart beat out of my chest at his touch. "Buddy Holly. The old folks love it."

"I like the way you sing it. Maybe you can sing it to me later."

Terry blushed at my flirtatious compliment, continuing to pat my back. People gave us weird, questioning looks. The bartender, George, in particular, stared at us, making me want to slide under the bar and disappear. Terry didn't stop, though, running his hand up and down the middle of my back, culminating at the nape of my neck. I pushed Terry's arm away, afraid people would get the wrong idea, even if it was the right idea. "You shouldn't touch me in public," I said. "People will get the wrong idea."

"I'll leave," he said, subtle irritation in his voice.

"You don't have to leave."

"Don't want people to talk, do we?" Terry walked off, heading to the corner where he typically sat and played. He picked up his guitar and left the pub, not looking back.

Although tempted to go after him, I remained sitting on my stool.

I didn't want people to think we were together in that kind of way. Instead, I gulped down my beer. George immediately poured me another. Maybe Terry's mother was right, and I wasn't strong enough for "this type of relationship." I wasn't prepared to answer questions about us or my sexuality. I was nothing but a coward.

Old music from the jukebox played, making me immediately think of Terry as I sipped my beer. I sat there until closing time.

"Are you going to stay here all night?" George asked me, wiping down the bar as the last group of people left.

"I can help you clean up," I offered.

"That won't be necessary," Terry said, unexpectedly standing behind me. "Go home, George. I'll finish up here."

"Sure," George said. "See you tomorrow. Have a good night. Relax, guys. I won't out you. That's not my style."

"Goodnight, George," Terry said. "Don't worry. He's cool. I shouldn't have left like that. It's not fair, is it?"

"No, it's not fair," I said, swallowing hard.

In the mood to dance, I went to the jukebox and selected a Billie Holiday song. As *I'll Be Seeing You* played, I made my way back to him. "Just one song," I said, taking his hand in mine. He kissed my lips, pulling me so close to him there was no space between us. "I love you. I never want to say goodbye."

"Ssh. Just dance."

We continued to hold each other even after the song finished. Terry suggested we leave to go back to his place. As I undressed, Terry started another fire. "You should really try to play hard to get," he laughed as I knelt beside him, already hard and ready to go.

"There's no time for that," I said, lifting his shirt over his head. As he removed his jeans and underwear, I discovered he was as hard as I was. I tackled him to the floor, pinning his arms over his head, pushing his legs open with my knee. He tried to wrestle me, but I won the battle.

"I told you you had skinny arms," I said, gripping his wrists, rubbing my cock against his.

"Maybe I let you win." Terry hooked his legs around my back as my tongue reached farther in his mouth. I broke away from him, my hands still firmly around his wrists as I planted kisses along his collarbone and all over his chest, down to his stomach. His cock stood at attention, just waiting for me. He giggled as I looked up at him, licking his shaft like a lollipop, culminating at the tip. "I love it when you do that."

He placed his hands on the back of my head, pushing me down on him, guiding me just the way he wanted it. As I achieved the right rhythm, he relaxed on his back, enjoying himself.

I sucked each ball, rubbing the tip of his cock with my thumb. He propped himself on his elbows, his eyes glued to me. He bit down on his bottom lip, making some sounds I'd never heard before. "There's lube by my bed," he said, breathing heavily. "I want you to do it. Go on… "

I got up and fetched the tube on his nightstand, hoping I'd have more success tonight.

"Don't be nervous," he said as I squeezed the clear liquid on my fingers. "I'm relaxed, so you relax." He opened his legs wide, allowing me easy access. I pressed my thumb against his entrance, circling it around and around. Coated with lube, I pushed the top half in him. "Holy shit!" Terry gasped. Afraid I hurt him, I quickly withdrew. "I wasn't expecting that." He took a deep breath. "How about you just start with a finger?"

"Yeah, okay. Sorry."

More nervous than before, I hesitated before bringing a finger back to him. Terry distracted me as he played with himself, waiting for me to make a move. I enjoyed watching him masturbate.

"Go on," he said. "I'm ready."

Finally, my finger made its way inside him. Terry moaned my name as I added another finger, stretching him. He liked my fingers in him, even as I added a third. Eventually, I gathered up enough courage to try it. With lots of lube on my cock, I bounced it against his entrance, just about ready. He groaned as I inched inside him. He was tight, closing in around me, his chest heaving in and out. I pushed all the way in him until there was no space between us. Terry gritted his teeth, his fists clenched on either side of him.

"Fuck," Terry muttered as I remained motionless inside him, partly afraid to move, mostly afraid I'd hurt him.

"Does it hurt?" I asked, my cock throbbing and pulsating inside him.

"No." His body trembled slightly.

"You feel good." I kissed his lips, beginning to move in him like he moved in me. He inhaled deeply, moaning as he exhaled into my mouth. He grasped clumps of my hair as I thrust back and forth, harder and faster. He wrapped his arms around me as I gained momentum.

My lips clamped down on his neck, coming harder than I'd ever come in my life. My body trembled in his arms as he pulled at my hair. Unexpectedly, he threw me on my stomach, doing it so fast I didn't have time to react. With my ass up in the air, I cried out in a combination of pain and ecstasy as he thrust hard inside me. Within seconds, he exploded, filling me. Limp in his arms, he held me upright against him, his hand on my cock. Cum trickled out of me as he slowly pulled out. He then re-inserted his cock, slipping it in and out.

"Fuck," I laughed, almost turned on all over again. "Let me do that to you next time."

Nodding against my neck, his lips turned into a smile. Emotionally and physically drained, I collapsed on my stomach, but Terry wanted to keep going, kissing the middle of my back. He kissed me all over, down to my ass. Round two was about to start minutes after round one ended. I found myself rejuvenated.

14

Chapter 14

Terry

Since we barely slept last night, I expected Scott to be late for breakfast again, but this morning I found him sitting with his mother and brother, along with another mother and her three daughters. The oldest stared at Scott dreamily, yearning for him. An unusual emotion soared through me, something I had never experienced before.

Jealousy.

Even though Scott looked rough with bags under his eyes, unshaven, and his dark hair in disarray, he still passed as a heartthrob. And because he had that "I don't give a shit" kind of attitude, I bet some girls found him even more irresistible.

The older girl sat beside Scott, talking non-stop, batting her eyelashes and twirling strands of hair around her finger. Indifferently, Scott sipped his coffee, struggling to keep his eyes open. As she blabbed to him, he rolled his eyes at me before turning his attention back to his coffee, forced to listen to this teen girl. Nancy Prescott always wanted to play matchmaker, and this girl seemed like the perfect daughter-in-law-to-be. With a fresh pot of coffee, I walked over to them to check things out.

"Good morning, Nancy," I said. "Would you like some more coffee?"

"Yes, please," she said with a smile. "Thank you. Terry, this is Tabitha, Kimberly, Raquel, and their mother, Linda."

"Nice to meet you," I said, even though I had probably already met them. I had met so many people during the summer, I couldn't remember everyone.

"Scott's taking Tabitha to the dance tonight," Nancy said. "They make a nice couple, don't they?"

I was never the violent type, but I had a desire to stab every person at the table.

"They're from Wellesley," Nancy continued, "which isn't too far from us."

"Terry doesn't care," Scott said.

"It's too bad you don't have a girlfriend, Terry," Nancy said, ignoring Scott's comment as I poured Linda a cup of coffee, my hand visibly shaking, my ears ringing.

"Stop it, Mom," Scott said. "You're embarrassing him."

"Are you okay?" Linda asked me.

"Uh... yeah... " I said with a fake smile. "I... uh... I... I have to go. Excuse me." With a pit in the middle of my stomach, I returned to the kitchen. Phonies made me sick, and I realized I was as big of a phony as Scott and his mother. My dad took the pot of coffee from me before I dropped it. "I need to lie down for a while."

"If I don't see you by lunchtime, I'm coming for you," he said. "I'm worried about you, you know."

"Well, don't." After tossing and turning for an hour, I fell asleep, waking up at one o'clock to mow the lawn. I didn't see Scott again until late afternoon.

With this new onset of painful jealousy, I sulked in Scott's room while he got ready for tonight's event. Overtired and cranky, I lay on Scott's bed in my worn-out jean shorts, jealousy burning my insides. Mike was already downstairs, socializing with his friends. "Do you like that girl?" I asked.

"What girl?"

"Tabitha."

"Are you serious?" he said, buttoning up the new red and white striped shirt that his mother bought him today. "You're not wearing that tonight, are you?"

"I don't feel like working or doing anything," I replied. I was never sick, but I contemplated telling my parents I was too sick to work tonight. They would never fall for my excuse, though, because they had an uncanny ability to know when I was lying. "I don't want to be there watching you pretend to be straight, pretending—"

"I'm not pretending to be anything," he interrupted me.

"Bullshit. Then why don't you tell that girl you're not interested? Who cares what your mother says? You're an adult."

"Have you met my mother? She'll keep going on and on, nagging me for the rest of the summer."

Sullenly, I wandered to the window, admiring the beautiful evening, one I would have preferred to spend with Scott and no one else.

"I hate seeing you like this. It's killing me."

"You and Tabitha and this charade; it's an example of things to come," I said. "You're going to find a girl, whether it's Tabitha or someone else, settle down, have a couple of kids, and forget all about me. This summer will be like it never happened. My mother's right; you're not strong enough."

"I don't know what you want from me." Annoyed and angry, he backed away from me. "This date is nothing. I don't even know her. I've told you a hundred times that I'm just doing it to make my mother happy so she'll shut up. Stop being so presumptuous."

"It's not fair. I want to be the one dancing with you, so, yeah, I'm jealous. I'm so jealous I can't see straight." With tears stupidly falling, I threw myself back on his bed. On my stomach, I rested my head on my folded arms.

Scott sat beside me and ran his hand all the way down my back and to the waist of my shorts. "Yeah, it's not fair," he said. "I could never forget you. I'll be thinking about you all night. Don't make me feel guilty. I promise I'll save a dance for you."

"I'll be waiting for you," I said as he patted my back.

"You look hot in these shorts." He kissed my bare shoulder.

"You're really something. That's why I'm going to miss you. I think I could spend the rest of my life with you."

He traced the waist of my shorts with his fingers, slipping them inside. As he bent down to kiss my shoulder again, I rolled over to face him. I reached up and pressed my hand on the back of his neck, pushing him down to kiss his mouth. As our kisses grew more and more intense, he yanked my shorts and underwear off in one tug.

"Are you crazy?" I said, shedding his clothes.

"A little. Turn over." He rolled me over before I reacted.

My eyes turned to the door, making sure I locked it so I could enjoy Scott's fingers inside me. Instead of lube, which was under the bed in my cottage, he spit on his hand, using his salvia. He grunted, pushing inside me, practically forcing his way in. He wasn't as gentle and cautious as the first time. I gritted my teeth and accepted the pain.

"Ssh," he said in my ear, thrusting in and out.

A new kind of pain seared through me, but I didn't tell him to stop. I liked it. I gripped the sheets, burying my head in the pillow. It was intense, the way Scott's lips clamped down on my neck, thrusting harder and faster. Scott came so hard inside me, he bit down on my neck, almost breaking the skin. But he didn't stop. He flipped me onto my back and scooted down my body, taking my cock in his mouth. I held his head, guiding him until I climaxed in his mouth.

"I promise I'll save a dance or two for you tonight." he said, peering up at me. His words didn't make a difference.

I left his room, escaping before anyone saw me. Depressed, I took another nap before dragging myself to the inn. My parents gave me that disapproving look they'd been giving me all summer. As music played, my eyes focused on Scott and that girl. Nancy gushed with pride, as if she had hand-picked a daughter-in-law-to-be. As I stood at the back table, Scott's eyes met mine and he stuck out his tongue at me, rolling his eyes, turning his attention back to his mother and Tabitha. She was pretty, wearing a sleeveless pale pink dress with spaghetti straps, her long dark hair hanging down her bare back.

"Don't worry," my mother whispered to me, transferring a case of Coke into my arms. "He's not interested in her."

"How can you tell?"

"I've got eyes, don't I? I'm not so sure about Nancy, though. She thinks she found her future daughter-in-law."

"I was thinking the same thing," I laughed. "Mom, does it bother you that I'm gay?" I asked, arranging the cans of Coke in the bowl of ice on the table.

"Don't be silly."

"Does it?" I persisted.

"No, it doesn't bother me as much as it'll bother some people in this world. I have to say, though, I was hoping for grandchildren."

"Sorry." At twenty, having kids was the farthest thing from my mind.

"Don't apologize," she said. "I never want you to feel bad or sorry for who you are. You've always been such a carefree spirit. I want you to stay that way."

With the sodas all sorted out, I turned back around to find Scott dancing with Tabitha. My heart sank. "That should be me out there," I told my mother before storming off.

In the kitchen, I dug out a beer from the back of the fridge, my dad's secret hiding spot. He didn't allow alcohol in the kitchen, but my dad always left a six-pack or two hidden in the back. My heart hurt in the worst way.

After two more beers, I needed something to do to keep myself distracted, so I feverishly cleaned the kitchen, from the fridge to the countertops to the floor. As I shined the stainless steel countertops for the second time, Scott walked into the kitchen, holding a lilac he picked from a bush outside. We had rows and rows of lilac bushes, so one flower wouldn't be missed. Smiling, I took the lilac from him. He didn't hesitate, leading me in a dance to a song that played in the adjoining restaurant.

"This is risky," I said, not pulling away from him, still holding the lilac.

"Everyone is busy out there. I tired Tabitha out. I want to stay with you tonight."

I nodded against his head. As the second dance played, Scott kissed my neck, culminating with a kiss on my lips. He slipped his tongue in my mouth, grasping clumps of my hair. The harder he pulled at my hair, the louder I moaned.

"Scott?"

Scott instantly pulled away from me as if I had some kind of infectious disease. "Tabitha," Scott's voice shook, as taken aback as I was. "What are you doing here?"

"Looking for you," she answered. "You disappeared. What are you doing?"

"N... n... nothing," he lied in a not-so-convincing way.

"Nothing? I saw you kissing *him*." She pointed to me like I was a dirty dog. "That's... that's *gross.*"

"I don't know what you saw," Scott said, "but we weren't doing anything."

"I saw *you*," she insisted as I attempted to leave the kitchen.

"We're shutting down soon," I said. "If you want one more dance, I suggest you get back out there."

"I don't dance with queers," she said in disgust. "I'm going to bed. Goodnight, Scott."

Just that word alone caused knots in my stomach. Tabitha ran out of the kitchen while Scott and I stood there frozen. I wondered what she would tell everyone, particularly her mother and Nancy. Scott looked as though he was about to pass out. We both avoided each other's eyes as I silently left the kitchen to help clean up for the night.

I don't dance with queers, the words echoed in my head. Ashamed, mostly because we were caught, I gathered up a bunch of dirty dishes and returned to the kitchen, discovering Scott had left without a word.

Before going to bed, I took a shower, the scene with Tabitha playing over and over in my mind. Shampoo spilled into my eyes as more shameful tears came. Distraught, I didn't even dry off as I crawled into bed, afraid Scott's summer was over, and I'd find him gone come morning.

Despite everything, I fell into a deep sleep, dreaming of a naked Scott in my bed, touching and kissing me. "Terry," Scott whispered in my ear. I realized I wasn't sleeping or dreaming, sensing his breath and naked body close to mine.

"Scott," I gasped, finding the real Scott hovering over me in the dark. "How'd you get in here?"

"Through the window. I popped the screen out."

"You shouldn't be here."

"I want to be here. If Tabitha says anything, I'll deny it. It's her word against ours, right?"

"I'm afraid people will believe her over us. We're always together."

"I'm sorry, Terry." He pressed his body against mine. "I'll never go out with a girl again. Lucky for you, I dance with queers."

I laughed as Scott scooted down my body, kicking all the blankets to the floor. My knees knocked against his head as he took my cock eagerly in his mouth. I held the back of his head, pushing him harder on my cock, so hard he gagged. With my cock in his mouth, he looked up at me, his eyes smiling and laughing. Tabitha seemed like forever ago.

As my cock slid in and out of his mouth, he reached up, squeezing my nipples. Grasping clumps of hair, I yanked his head back, forcing him to release me. Our lips rejoined, his body between my legs.

His fingers circled my entrance, already lubed up. My ass lifted off the bed as he pulled me to him. He bit his bottom lip, concentrating as he entered me, little by little. My toes curled against his lower back as his cock throbbed inside me.

Still inside me, he maneuvered his way onto his back, urging me to ride him. My knees dug into his sides as I bounced slowly up and down. We held each other tightly, my lips against his neck, his fingers clawing my back. He pushed me on my back again and thrust hard, coming deep inside me, so deep we both cried out in a mixture of pain and ecstasy.

Around two thirty in the morning, we both crashed from exhaustion. Scott fell asleep first, lying on his stomach, all the blankets in a heap on the floor. Two more weeks. That's how much time we had left together. "Go to sleep, Terry," he muttered, hugging his pillow.

I kissed his shoulder and closed my eyes, wondering if sleep would ever come.

"I think I could spend the rest of my life with you, too," he said. "Goodnight."

I couldn't have fallen asleep to a better thought.

* * *

Once again, I had overslept, waking to a knock on my door. Annoyed, Scott kicked me, forcing me to get up to answer the door. Automatically,

I assumed it was one of my parents since they were growing more and more impatient with me, tired of me shrugging off my responsibilities. "I'm coming!" I shouted, dragging my ass out of bed. I slipped on a pair of shorts and staggered to the door, half asleep.

At six in the morning, I opened the door to find the picture-perfect Nancy Prescott standing on my front stoop, a dour expression on her face, one that I had never seen before. There were no signs of a phony, unnaturally chipper Nancy. Her unhappy expression told me that Scott's date last night spilled the beans.

"Nancy," I said, barely able to disguise my fear. "Is everything okay?" I played dumb and naïve. "Can I help you with anything?"

"I know he's here," she stated, straight to the point. "Go get him."

"Who?"

"Don't play stupid, Terry."

Responding to her voice, Scott appeared beside me, fully dressed. His mother glared at him like he committed a heinous crime. She didn't say a word, her eyes full of anger and disgust, loathing her own son. Unexpectedly, she slapped him hard against his cheek, leaving a handprint.

"What was that for?" Scott asked, stunned, holding his cheek. "I didn't do anything."

But we both knew why she slapped him. I stepped in front of him before she slapped him again. "Don't," I said. "He did nothing wrong."

"You stay away from him," she said to me through gritted teeth, her voice seething with anger.

Scott stood there meekly, dumbfounded and petrified, not the Scott I had come to know this summer. He always told me he was afraid of his parents finding out, afraid of what they'd do to him. Now I understood why.

"Let's go, Thomas," she said. "Now."

"He did nothing wrong," I called to her as they headed back to the inn. "Nothing happened, you know."

"Stay away from him!"

But Scott said nothing. He didn't even look back at me. Afraid our love affair was really over, I ran to the bathroom and threw up. *It can't be over. I'm not ready.*

15

Chapter 15

Scott

Bright and early in the morning, my mother showed up at Terry's door. No doubt Tabitha squealed and told her she saw me kissing Terry in the kitchen. As much as I denied it, Tabitha couldn't deny what she saw. I also couldn't deny the fact Terry and I had been together most of the night and that he left a giant hickey on my neck. I hadn't seen it yet, but judging by his kisses last night, I was sure he left a mark or two. My mother hadn't slapped me like that since I was eleven years old after I tore my good pants climbing a tree. I was supposed to wear my play clothes whenever I climbed trees, and I climbed a lot of them.

Instead of sending me to my room, my mother took me to her room to "give me a talking to." That's what she used to say to me whenever I did something wrong. Prepared for a vicious scolding, she slapped me again. With only seconds in between, she brought her hand to my other cheek. "Sit down," she said.

With my cheeks burning, I sat on the edge of the bed.

"I thought we raised you better than this," she reprimanded me as I sat there like a naughty little boy about to get a spanking. "What's wrong with you, Thomas?" My mother only called me Thomas when she was angry and disappointed with me. I had never seen her this angry. "Do you know how unnatural that is? It's not normal. It's sick."

Ashamed, I looked down at the floor. She made me feel dirty and immoral. I hated myself, more so because I was foolish enough to get caught. I loved Terry and that would never change, no matter what she said, no matter how she made me feel.

"Just because you have these feelings, doesn't mean you should act on them. Look at me when I'm speaking to you, Thomas."

Preparing myself for another slap, I reluctantly lifted up my chin to meet her green eyes.

"Did you hear me? You could have any girl. Why settle on a boy who's nothing more than a deadbeat hippie who will probably end up living in some hippie commune? Do you want to end up in a place like that?" Terry was anything but a so-called "deadbeat."

"You know nothing about Terry," I said.

"I know you're better than him." She couldn't have been more wrong. "I'm so glad this summer is almost over, then you can put this all behind you and get on with your life. We can forget this ever happened, and you never have to see him again. I won't tell your father about this. It'll kill him and destroy his friendship with Frankie. You're going to stay away from that boy, you hear me?"

I'd never stay away from Terry as long as I was there.

"Do you hear me, Thomas?"

"I hear you," I said.

"Now go wash up. We're going out for brunch. Wear a bandana or something around your neck to hide that thing. You're a disgrace."

With my head down, I shuffled out of my mother's room in shame. I went straight to my bathroom and into the shower. As the water beat down on me, I pounded my fists against the tiled shower wall, bawling my eyes out.

* * *

My mother kept Mike and I busy all day, between museums, the arcade, and a spur of the moment shopping spree. She must have felt guilty for slapping me because she bought me the expensive sneakers I'd wanted. She also splurged on ice cream and slushies and other treats. By nighttime, the three of us made it back just in time for the giant bonfire.

"Remember what I said," my mother said to me as my eyes drifted to Terry who was playing his guitar in front of the fire. All I thought about was getting close to him. Our eyes met for half a second. Tabitha and her sisters weren't around, or if they were, they were avoiding the Prescott family. My mother tensed as Susan Lachance approached us. Since we arrived, my mother and Susan spoke very little to each other. My mother saved her words for members of her own social class, and Susan and Frankie weren't part of that class.

"Hi, Scott, I haven't seen you all day," Susan said. "What have you been up to?"

"He's just going to bed. Aren't you, Scottie?" my mother said. "He's had a migraine all day. Go ahead, Scottie, go to bed."

On the verge of puking, vomit coated my teeth as I headed back to the inn. I glanced over my shoulder, observing my mother gravitate to another rich bitch gossiper. I realized I'd rather die than end up like her.

Cooped up in my room, I took out my sketchbook and attempted to draw. Uninspired and unmotivated, I chucked my sketchbook across the room. I turned on the radio, catching the end of the Red Sox game. At least they were winning. At some point, I must have dozed off because I didn't hear Mike come in.

In the middle of the night, I woke up, my body craving Terry's. I popped the screen out of Terry's window again and climbed into his cottage. He bolted upright, sensing my presence. He jumped off his bed and ran to me, throwing his arms around me. "I'm sorry about all this," he said, hugging me tightly.

"It's not your fault. There's nothing to apologize for."

"What about your dad?" He pulled away from me, placing his hands on my shoulders.

"She won't tell him, but I'm supposed to stay away from you. That won't happen." With my arms around him, I breathed into his neck, taking in his scent. "I can't stay the night."

"I know. Someday we'll wake up together every morning."

I loved that thought.

In an embrace, we collapsed on his bed in each other's arms. We kissed each other long, hard, and deep. I wrapped my legs around his waist. Usually, we'd take our time, savoring each other, taking breaks only to resume again. Tonight was different. Minutes after Terry finished, I put my clothes back on. Terry sat there, chewing on his bottom lip, noticeably sad.

"What will your mother do if she finds out you've been with me?" Terry asked.

"Maybe slap me again. She won't tell my dad, that's for sure. She's as afraid as I am."

On my way to the door, I noticed Terry's sketchbook on his table. I stopped to open it. "You're going to draw at two a.m.?" he asked.

"No, I'm going to write down my phone number and address in case you don't have it."

"You're not leaving tomorrow, are you?" he asked, approaching me. He patted my back as I wrote down my phone number, home address, and university address.

"No, not for another two weeks."

"Good... because I'm not ready to say goodbye."

We kissed goodnight and I reluctantly left, sneaking back into my room at two thirty in the morning.

* * *

After a tubing adventure with Mike and Frankie, we sat around the picnic table eating a late lunch, everyone except Terry. I hadn't seen him since early this morning. Terry was helping out in the kitchen because the sous chef quit.

"Dad!" Mike said excitedly. My dad unexpectedly showed up a week early. Either it was a surprise or my mother called him, maybe to go home early. If she had told him what had happened with me and Terry, I would have known it. He seemed like his usual self, so I knew she hadn't said a word about it.

"Hi, Scottie," he said. "Have you been behaving?"

My mind raced, and I didn't know what to say. What did he mean by that?

"Yes," my mother said on my behalf. "We've all had a lovely summer." My mother went up to him and kissed his cheek. "It's good to see you, Tom. We've missed you."

I wasn't so sure I missed him. His arrival meant we were all going home soon. *This is the end*, an unbearable thought.

"Hey, Scottie, where are you off to?" my dad asked as I walked away.

"I have a migraine," I said.

"You're still getting those?"

Since puberty, I'd often get these whopping headaches. The doctor said they were migraines brought on by stress and anxiety. A bad migraine could wipe me out for days.

On my freshly made bed, I found a folded piece of paper on my pillow, the size of one of Terry's sketches. I unfolded it and discovered a black and white sketch of the two of us, bare chested, my arm around his waist. On the bottom of the page was a bunch of hearts, Terry's name underneath them. With tears in my eyes, I folded it back up and stuck it in my sketchbook.

* * *

Debilitated with a migraine, I stayed in bed. Any noise and sunlight nauseated me. Mike brought me food, which I hardly touched. Migraines zapped my usual ravenous appetite. On the third day in bed, I wasn't expecting Terry to show up. "Your parents and Mike went into town," he said, approaching me on my bed. "No one knows I'm here. Is it okay if I stay with you for a little while?"

I nodded, my migraine not nearly as bad as it was a day ago.

"You look like you could use a shower," he said. "Come on. I'll take one with you."

Showering with Terry always made me feel better. In the shower, he stood behind me, kissing my neck, sliding a washcloth between my butt cheeks. "Please don't give me any more hickeys," I said.

"Sorry about that," he said, smiling against my neck.

After our shower, we quickly dried off and ended up naked on top of the covers on my bed. "Are you up for this?" Terry asked.

"You're just what I need." He circled my entrance with his fingers.

"You want me to lick you?"

"Yes."

He opened me up with his fingers, sticking his tongue there, letting his saliva dribble all over it. He alternated between his finger and tongue. I loved the way he licked and fingered me. "Wait," I said, resting my ankles on his shoulders. "I don't want to come yet."

Terry grunted against my lips, pushing hard in me. As much as it hurt, I didn't want him to stop. "Keep going," I urged him.

We both cried out, climaxing with an intensity we'd never experienced before. "Holy shit," Terry said, collapsing on top of my back. "That was crazy."

The door suddenly flung open. Terry and I turned our heads, both stunned to see my dad standing there. "What do you think you're doing?" My dad's booming voice scared the shit out of us. I saw my life flash before my eyes.

This can't be happening.

Shocked and terrified, Terry stumbled off me. As he went to run to the bathroom to retrieve his clothes, my dad charged toward him. He grabbed the back of his neck, swung him around, and punched him so hard in his face he fell to the floor.

"Dad!"

"I had a feeling you were a faggot, but I let Scottie hang out with you, anyway," my dad said, picking him up off the floor to punch him again.

"Stop!" I begged, quickly pulling up my shorts as he kicked Terry on the floor. "Dad, stop it. Stop... you're hurting him!"

"Shut up, Scottie," my dad said. "How dare you corrupt my son, you piece of shit."

"Stop it!" I shouted to him as he kicked him again and again. My heart hurt, hearing my dad call the most amazing man in the world "a piece of shit." Before he touched Terry again, I shoved him hard, almost knocking him to the floor. "Don't you ever touch him!"

"What's going on in here?" Frankie Lachance asked, standing in the doorway.

"Your faggot of a son took advantage of my boy," my dad said.

Terry lay on the floor, naked, shaken, and disoriented, his nose bleeding. I grabbed the nearest pair of shorts I could find and helped him put them on.

"What did you do to *my* boy?" Frankie asked my dad, angry and stunned.

"He should be shot for what he was doing to Scottie," my dad said.

"I'm so sorry, Terry," I said to him as his body shook.

"Get your hands off him," my dad snarled as I helped Terry into a shirt.

"I'm sorry," Terry whispered to me, blood dripping from his nose. I held him in my arms, trying to get him to stop shaking.

"Terry!" Susan Lachance shrieked, running to him.

"He was raping my son," my dad said. "I should call the police and have him arrested."

Raping my son?

"Dad, he wasn't raping me."

"I knew what you were doing, you disgusting monster," my dad spat at Terry.

"Get off my property," Frankie said to my dad. "Terry's a good boy and look what you did to him. Get out before *I* call the police."

"We were leaving, anyway. Boys, pack your things. Now!"

Just then, I realized Mike was there. Frankie and I helped Terry to his feet.

"I... I'm sorry," Terry stammered. "It's going to be okay."

I didn't feel like anything was ever going to be okay again. Terry's father pulled him away from me, forcing me to let go. He looked over his shoulder once as his parents walked him out of my room.

"Five minutes," my dad ordered us, glaring at me, repulsed, his fists clenched at his sides. He and my mother walked out, leaving Mike and I alone to pack our suitcases. Mike retrieved his suitcase from the closet and threw it on the bed.

"Why'd you have to ruin everything?" he said as I tossed my clothes haphazardly in my suitcase. "You always ruin everything. Why were you kissing Terry? Scottie, you were kissing him like boys kiss girls. Boys don't do that."

I stopped packing and looked at him in horror. "How did you know that?" I asked.

"I saw you. It's my room, too."

"I thought you went to town with Mom and Dad."

"We did, but then I got bored and wanted to go swimming. That's when I saw him doing those things to you. He was hurting you, so I got Dad."

"You got Dad?" I repeated incredulously.

"You were crying and... and... "

"He wasn't hurting me." Water blurred my vision. I had never hated Mike this much in my entire life. "You ruined my life. We're no longer brothers, you got that?" I had disowned him as a brother at least a hundred times in his life. This time I really meant it.

"What was he doing to you?" he persisted with more questions.

"I'm not talking to you ever again."

"Why were you crying like that?"

"Shut up, Mike. You know shit. I could fucking kill you. I fucking hate you."

"That's the last time I'm helping you."

I nearly leaped across the room to strangle him to death. It was a good thing he left the room. Our dad was already in the car, ready to go, clutching the steering wheel when I lugged my suitcase and duffel bag out. My mother wasn't too far behind, carrying her purse and make-up bag.

"Get in the car, Scottie," she said, putting on a fake smile in case anyone was watching us.

Tears blurred my vision again as I scanned the area for Terry. A simple wave goodbye would have been nice.

"Put your things in the trunk and get in," my dad said with the car window down. Sniffing back my tears, I did as he said. "You're going to forget about him and this summer. Stop crying like a pansy."

Staring out the window, I shed a tear or two, biting my lip to fight off more tears. Just as my dad was about to pull out of the parking lot, Terry came out of nowhere, sprinting toward the car in his bare feet.

He ran so fast, he wasn't paying attention to the ground and tripped and fell.

"Stop the car," I said. "Stop!" When my dad didn't stop, I opened the door and tumbled out. I ran to Terry and helped him to his feet. He was sobbing hysterically, dried blood caked under his nose.

"It's going to be okay," I said, hugging him. Usually he was the one reassuring and consoling me. "You have my address. Write me, okay? Write me all the time."

He nodded against my shoulder. "I promise I'll write you every day. I love you, Scott. Don't forget me."

"I'll never forget you," I said as a car door slammed.

"Scottie, get in the car," my dad said. "Let go of him," my dad warned Terry.

"I love you, too," I whispered in his ear.

Clutching the back of my collar, my dad yanked me to my feet. I couldn't look at Terry's crying eyes anymore. It killed me. With my head down, I followed my dad back to the car. As the station wagon sped away from the Lachance property, I held my face in my hands, sobbing quietly.

"It's best to forget him and move on," my mother said. "Put it all behind you."

"Stop your bullshit crying," my dad said. "You're nothing like him. You're not a hippie beatnik faggot. Leave it to Frankie to raise a kid like that."

Mike leaned over the front seat to turn up the radio, probably to drown me out. My family rarely ever saw me cry, but I was too distraught to give a shit. My entire body hurt, not just my heart.

16

Chapter 16

Terry

Minutes after the Prescott car drove off, I sat there in the dirt, sobbing like a lovesick, heart-broken fool. Guests stopped doing whatever they were doing to watch the owner's son completely lose his mind. I wanted to tell everyone to fuck off, but that wasn't my style. I wasn't one to yell or tell people off.

"Terry, let him go," my dad had said as I paced around our small kitchen, my face and body sore from Tom Prescott's punches and kicks. My parents lived in an adjoining house to the inn. When I was growing up, I used to live there, too, but I moved into one of the cottages when I was seventeen. "I knew something like this was going to happen," my dad added as I bit my fingernails, a nasty habit I had overcome years ago. Those words were the last words I wanted to hear. And I couldn't just "let him go."

"Fuck it," I said before bolting out of the house to the Prescott station wagon. I didn't want to let him go. Scott didn't want to let me go, either. He jumped out of a moving car to get to me. At least I got to hug him one last time.

My parents were always there for me, including right now as the Prescott family disappeared down the road. At first, I shrugged my parents off as they crouched down in front of me, attempting to console me yet again. "Come on, Terry, it's going to be okay," my dad said, lifting me to my feet for the second time that day.

My legs were like jelly, so wobbly I could barely walk. On one side of me, my mother held her arm around my waist while my dad draped an arm over my shoulder, standing on the other side of me. My parents sat me down at their kitchen table as I continued to sob. My mother took a cool washcloth to my face, wiping the dirt off. I pushed her hand away, taking the washcloth from her. Instead of cleaning my face, I cried into the cloth.

My dad placed a hand on my shoulder."I'm sorry, kiddo." He hadn't called me "kiddo" since I was fourteen. "I guess I didn't realize how crazy you were about each other."

"It's not over," my mother said in another useless attempt to cheer me up. "What you have is real."

My mother's words were futile. With such a broken heart, I convinced myself I'd die without him. For days, I stayed in my cottage, too despondent to move. I always looked forward to going back to college, but I wasn't looking forward to anything right now. My mother would leave a tray of food outside my door on the front stoop, but I couldn't eat. Sleeping was hard, too, even though I spent most of my time in bed, only getting up to go to the bathroom. A sense of sadness and complete emptiness overwhelmed me.

Without my permission, my mother entered my cottage. In my pajamas, I sullenly stared out the window. I hadn't taken a shower since Scott left a week ago, the day Tom Prescott caught us in a compromising position in bed. I couldn't believe he accused me of rape.

Thinking back on that day, I was certain I locked the door, so how could his dad have gotten into the room? Maybe Scott left the key somewhere and Mike got his hands on it? Or maybe Mike had a key I didn't know about. Was twelve-year-old Mike the one who caught us in bed together? Was this all Mike's fault? I had a hard time blaming a twelve-year-old boy who may have seen something he didn't understand.

"You didn't knock," I said to my mother.

"I'm just making sure you're still alive. Should I be worried? This has been going on for five days."

"Stop worrying about me."

"I can't help it. I'm your mother. Shouldn't you be packing? It might do you some good to get up and do something."

In two days I was leaving for college, my final year. Never one to stray too far from home, next year would be a rude awakening for me, stationed somewhere in a third world country with the Peace Corps for a two-year stint. During that time, my parents would have to rely on someone else to do all the gardening and entertaining.

"I know it's hard." My mother patted my back as tears intermittently fell. "You were always so sensitive. I'm not saying that's a bad thing, but it can be a bit of a burden at times, can't it? You wear your heart on your sleeve. You love everyone and everything. It's so hard seeing you like this. It's not you."

"Because I've never been in love," I choked. "My heart's never been ripped out of my chest and stomped on. I'll never love anyone else."

"That's how you feel right now, but you'll love others."

"You said it's not over," I sniffed.

"I'm just saying there are other men out there if it doesn't work out for you and Scott."

"I don't want any other man. Go away, Mom. You're not helping. Just leave me alone."

"Okay, I'm leaving. I don't mean to be a nag, but when do you plan on packing?"

"Leave me alone," I reiterated. Packing was the farthest thing from my mind. She patted my back one more time and kissed my cheek.

"I'll check on you later. Remember, I'm the only mother you've got. It's my job to worry. Love you."

"Yeah, love you, too," I said as she left.

Within the hour, I forced myself out of bed and tossed random pieces of clothing in my suitcases. As I packed, I spotted my open sketchbook where Scott had scribbled his contact information. For an artist, he had terrible handwriting. His terrible handwriting brought a smile to my lips.

Although he only left a week ago, it felt like forever. I had to talk to him one more time before I left for college. I just hoped I'd catch him before he left. Since I couldn't call long distance from my cottage, I went to the inn, hoping my parents weren't around to talk me out of calling him. Scanning the area, I didn't see my parents anywhere, only a few guests milling around the lobby. My heart thumped out of my chest as I sat at the front desk, holding the receiver in my hand, praying Scott would answer the phone and not his parents. Lately I had the worst luck in the world; Mike answered the phone. "Hi, Mikey, how are you? It's Terry."

"I know it's you," Mike responded. "You shouldn't be calling here."

"Is Scott there?"

"Nope," he said with a bite to his voice, like I was a jerk when just a few weeks ago he was begging me to take him tubing.

"Can you tell me if he's left for college?"

Mike paused before responding. I thought he had hung up, but I didn't hear a dial tone. "Yeah, he left. He doesn't want to see you. If you call here again, I'm telling my dad."

"Sorry to bother you," I said, swallowing my tears.

"Get lost... freak."

Click. Blinking, I squeezed the water out of my eyes. *Freak*. *Queer*. He didn't call me queer, but I knew that's what he was thinking.

"Oh, Terry," my mother said, appearing in the doorway.

Whenever I needed them, my parents were always there. Years later, I'd realize how lucky I was to have such supportive, loving parents. Scott wasn't so lucky. My mother came to me and I fell into her arms, sobbing until there were no tears left to shed. I never wanted to fall in love again. It hurt way too much.

17

Chapter 17

Scott

Within the first month of college, I wrote Terry at least a dozen letters. After each letter, I expected one in return but none ever came. A few more months passed and another dozen letters mailed with no response. I didn't understand. He told me he'd write. He promised me. Terry wasn't a liar or a heartbreaker, so my dad must have scared the shit out of him. Something must have happened.

My roommate, Dustin, a southern boy with overprotective and overbearing parents, took advantage of his newfound freedom. He monopolized our room every Saturday night. He'd come home from a party, drunk, and with a girl. Not interested in watching or listening to a heterosexual couple get it on, I'd leave and spend my nights in the library.

"What's with you?" my roommate asked as I sulked on the top bunk, homesick, missing my room, my bed, and my old friends. And, of course, there was Terry. As hard as I tried, I couldn't get him out of my mind.

"Nothing," I replied.

"Missing someone?" he prodded.

"Maybe."

"Hey, you never told me you had a girl at home." Because Dustin liked girls so much, his assumption didn't surprise me. I'd never admit that my "missing someone" was a man.

"I had someone, but not anymore."

"Aw, man, I'm sorry. I know what it's like. I got my heart broken once." Dustin could talk anyone's ear off, so I prepared myself for a story. "Her name was Evelyn Wright, and she was beautiful. She had these big brown eyes and long blond hair. God, she was beautiful… " His voice trailed off, possibly envisioning his drop-dead gorgeous ex-girlfriend in bed with him. "And then she cheated on me with Earle Carter, the football quarterback. Did yours cheat on you, too?"

"No," I said.

"Then what happened?"

"My parents don't approve."

"Yeah, my parents didn't approve of me and Karen Feingold, either," he said. "Because we're Baptist and she's Jewish. There aren't many Jews in South Carolina, but I found one. Are your parents racist? Is that the problem?"

"I guess you could say they're prejudiced," I said, not prepared to go into any further details.

Dustin, trying to be a nice guy, set me up with a few girls. Making out with girls wasn't so bad, but I craved something more, something girls could never give me.

After two years of no response from Terry, I gave up and stopped writing to him. By that point, he was somewhere in the world with the Peace Corps. I had to face the fact I'd never see him again… all because Mike fucked everything up.

As my college years wore on, I satisfied my needs by finding men in various clubs, clubs I'd never find Terry in. Whenever I hooked up with a guy, satisfaction only lasted for ten or twenty minutes. Shortly after leaving the club, guilt and shame overtook me. Half the time, I didn't even know their names.

In the early to mid-eighties, gay men started to die from this mysterious virus known as the "gay plague." As this virus spread, I stopped having sex with men altogether. Some people thought homosexuals deserved to die, my parents included. They'd watch the news on TV and shake their heads, annoyed when anyone even mentioned it. One time, my mother had the nerve to say to me, "See what we saved you from? Is this the life you'd want to lead?"

I had no response to that bullshit comment.

Not long after the first HIV test came out in 1985, I had a blood test, travelling a hundred miles from home to have it. I didn't want to take a chance and have it done by my own doctor, afraid people would find out. Although gay people weren't the only ones who contracted the disease, there was a stigma attached to it. Unless I was an IV drug user or needed a blood transfusion, there was only one other reason why I'd have such a blood test. When my negative results came in, I felt like I had a new lease on life.

Condoms were a safe option, but I decided to refrain from any kind of homosexual activity, convinced I'd get the disease and die a horrible death, scared and alone. So I swore off homosexuality... for a little while, anyway.

Some would say I was a hypocrite since I took a job at my dad's advertising firm after college. I always said I'd never work for him, that I didn't want to work sixty to eighty hours a week. I graduated magna cum laude from Rochester Tech and could have worked anywhere, but I had a fear of the unknown. Mike went in a totally different direction. He wanted nothing to do with business or advertising. Before he decided on teaching, he focused on football, girls, and partying. My parents had different expectations for him than for me.

Only a year after telling myself I'd never have sex with a man again, the twenty-one-year-old summer intern in my dad's firm, Ethan Kramer, caught my eye. Now twenty-five, I had been celibate for the past year. I was itching to get laid—by a guy—and Ethan Kramer was fuckable. He reminded me of Terry. Skinnier than Terry, his blue eyes were just as stunning but not as gray or big. His dirty blond hair was only slightly shorter than Terry's, the Terry I remembered, anyway.

I often wondered where Terry went during his two-year Peace Corps stint and what he was doing now. Despite the time lapse and the broken promises, my heart still ached for him. No one could ever take his place.

But I liked Ethan, and I caught his eye, too. He blushed whenever I smiled at him. His pink cheeks told me he liked me in a not-so-friendly kind of way, and he didn't turn me down when I offered to buy him a drink after work. In fact, he looked relieved that I asked him out. At first, I made it sound like a friendly gesture, two guys grabbing a beer after work, but we both knew it was something else. After our beers, we couldn't wait to go somewhere else.

Since I lived with my parents, saving up for a down payment for a house, I took Ethan to a motel. Ethan's shyness and nervousness made him even more irresistible. Seconds after I closed the door, I tore off his shirt, about to ravage him. I hadn't been with a guy in a damn long time.

"You can't tell anyone about this, okay?" I said in his ear, my hands fumbling with his belt. "My dad could ruin your career, you understand?"

"I won't tell anyone," he assured me.

In the middle of the room, I got down on my knees and undid his pants. He looked down at me with his big blue eyes, reminding me of someone else in so many ways.

"Is this okay?" I asked. Ethan nodded once, his eyes wide with anticipation. It was a nice cock. All I thought about was Terry, even as I sucked his dick. I tugged down his pants and underwear and pushed him on the bed. My lips trailed all the way down his torso before I undressed.

"I've never done this before," he said, watching me take off my shirt.

"What?"

"I've never done this before," he repeated as I dropped my pants. "So I'm a little nervous. Will it hurt?"

"It might," I said, rolling on a condom. I lubed him up good before entering him. He held his breath, wincing in pain. I thrust slowly back and forth, imagining Terry underneath me.

"Scott," Ethan said. "Hey, Scott, who are you thinking about right now?"

"Huh?"

"You're thinking about someone. Who is it?"

"I'm sorry," I said, pushing up on my hands. "Does it feel okay?"

"Yeah, I just wish I was him."

"I'm not thinking of anyone," I lied, but he saw right through me.

"He must have been very special."

Ignoring his last comment, I brought my lips to his, attempting to block Terry out. He was long gone, yet he kept popping up in my mind.

Ethan and I continued to see each other, becoming more than a one-night stand. In the beginning, we did a good job of hiding our relationship. Every now and again, Ethan's hand would brush against mine and he'd blush. When my dad found out he was gay, he immediately suspected there was something going on between us and nearly ended his internship. To prove there was nothing going on, I didn't balk when my mother set me up on a date with twenty-six-year-old Aimee Thomas, a recent Yale graduate. At twenty-six, some people in my mother's circle considered her an old maid. My mother, however, considered her the catch of the century.

Aimee was pretty and smart, a civil rights lawyer for the ACLU. I liked the liberal type. She wasn't as stuffy as her parents and not a Reagan supporter, which was good enough for me. The daughter of an associate Vice President of the advertising division of a pharmaceutical company my dad collaborated with, Aimee was everything my mother wanted in a daughter-in-law. Her parents also belonged to the same country club. Unlike her parents, Aimee was genuine and not stuck up. She was down to Earth and someone I could almost love. I realized she'd make a good wife and mother. She was the only woman I ever slept with. It was nice but not great. There was only one great.

18

Chapter 18

1990
Scott

Back in late 1980, I disowned Mike for six months, the longest I'd ever disowned him. Squealing to my dad was the worst thing he had ever done to me. Years later, Mike and I preferred to ignore the subject altogether rather than open old wounds.

Here we were, ten years later, at the country club celebrating Mike's college graduation. A slacker and hard-core partier, he graduated in the middle of his class from the University of Massachusetts. After earning a degree in education, he intended to teach middle school science. Mike and I couldn't have been more different. Science was always my worst subject.

Ever since his freshman year of high school, Mike couldn't wait to leave home. For the past two years, he supported himself working in various restaurants. I envied him because he had the balls to leave home while I still lived under my parents' thumb, working with my dad at his advertising firm. By living with my parents, I saved a lot of money, but was money all that important? It wasn't to Mike.

Aimee and I had been dating for two years now. Every day she expected me to pop the question, a question I wasn't sure I'd ever be able to ask anyone. Aimee loved me, something she told me multiple times a day. It wasn't fair of me to string her along, but I liked her and, to be honest, I was afraid to be single and alone. Torn between wanting a family and committing to a woman for the rest of my life, I couldn't decide if having a family was worth living a lie. If I had children, what kind of role model would I be? I wouldn't want my children to pretend to be someone they weren't.

Surrounded by his friends, celebrating this milestone, Mike didn't seem happy, distracted, repeatedly shifting his eyes in my direction. With my arm around Aimee's waist, I smiled and nodded at the rich bitches and asshole members of the club. My mother was the queen of this group of phonies. Mike wandered away from his friends, approaching me with two beers in his hands.

"Scott, can I talk to you for a minute?" Mike said. He handed me a beer, scanning the room suspiciously as if he was about to disclose some deep, dark secret.

"What the hell's wrong with you?" I asked.

"Come on," he said, leading me outside, away from all the guests.

"Are you okay? Are you sick or something? Got a girl pregnant?" I half-teased, but there was always the possibility. He loved women and always had a girlfriend or two.

"God, no. I'm fine." His eyes avoided mine as he took a big gulp of his beer. He was dying to tell me something. "I… uh… well… " he stammered, nervously raking his fingers through his dark hair.

"What is it, Mike? Just tell me," I said, growing more and more impatient.

He took a deep breath and spit it out. "Terry Lachance is here. He's in town for Memorial Day."

My hand shook, spilling half my beer at the mention of his name. No one ever mentioned any Lachance. It was like a bad word in our house. To my old man, Frankie Lachance was dead to him.

"His dad passed away," Mike said. My heart sank, filled with sorrow for Terry and his family. Terry and his mother must have been devastated. "He was a Korean vet, so the town's honoring him or something. I guess he was sort of a hero."

My dad never made it to Korea. He never told us why.

"The town's honoring him at the Memorial Day celebration. Pete told me. His brother's in the Boy Scouts." Pete was one of Mike's best friends. "Terry is accepting the award on his dad's behalf. I thought you'd want to know."

"Why?" I said, even though my heart fluttered in a way it hadn't fluttered in a very long time. "It was a long time ago. It doesn't matter anymore."

"Look, Scott. I was just a kid. I didn't understand." He squeezed my shoulder as my eyes wandered away from his, water slowly filling them no matter how hard I tried to fight the tears off.

"We were just kids. It was just a one-time thing... an experiment."

"You jumped out of a moving car to get to him. Don't tell me it was just an experiment."

"What do you expect me to do, huh? I wrote him all the time and he never wrote me back. I was an experiment to *him*."

"Maybe you should go and find out," he said, withdrawing his hand from my shoulder. "Tell him I said hi and I'm sorry. You know I'm sorry, right?" Mike paused, looking at me hard, waiting for my response. "If it was a one-time thing, an experiment, then why are you crying?"

"I'm not crying," I sniffed.

"I guess I'm just seeing things," he said, backing away from me. "There's a big parade downtown. The ceremony will be outside town hall next Saturday."

Terry Lachance is coming to town? Holy shit, I thought to myself. *I'm really going to give him a piece of my mind.* But I wasn't so sure I could face him again, not after all this time.

"Hey, Scottie, what are you doing out here all by yourself?" Aimee asked me, zapping me back to reality. At barely five foot two, she was beautiful, brilliant, and one hell of a lawyer. She could argue anyone to death. Dressed in a lavender blouse, white A-line skirt and matching white pumps, she approached me as I pondered my predicament.

"Huh?" I said, barely hearing what she said.

"What's wrong? You look like you've seen a ghost."

"I just needed some fresh air. I'm not feeling well. Maybe it was something I ate. Could your parents take you home?"

"I told you to stay away from the stuffed mushrooms. They never agree with you. I'll call you later to check on you." She kissed my cheek before returning to the party. She was a good person and loved me way more than I loved her. I didn't want to break her heart.

All week I thought about Terry, so much so I had a hard time focusing on my work. One part of me said I shouldn't go, that I should forget Mike even mentioned it, the other part said I had to go, that I had to face him again, at least to clarify some things.

Early Saturday morning, I paced around my room, imagining seeing Terry again after all this time. I abruptly stopped pacing to stare at the suit I intended to wear.

Should I or shouldn't I go?

Shit shit shit. I pulled at my hair. *What the fuck should I do?*

I decided to go in honor of Frankie. As I dressed, I wondered what Terry looked like now at thirty. I couldn't wait to see him.

* * *

The Boy Scouts led the annual Memorial Day parade with one boy holding the American flag and another boy holding the Boy Scouts flag. People lined the streets, watching the Scouts, local veterans, and the high school marching band make their way to their destination. I couldn't see Terry anywhere.

The parade culminated at Town Hall where I stood and waited the whole time. A row of folding chairs lined the front steps, a podium stationed in front of the double doors of the main entrance. State Representative John Langdon stood behind the podium, ready to give a speech. Six men sat in the chairs, everyone except Terry. Maybe Pete's kid brother was wrong, and I wasted an entire Saturday for nothing.

That's what I thought until I spotted a man, a man much younger than the others, arrive a few minutes later. Dressed in a light blue short-sleeved button-down shirt and dark blue jeans, the young man shook everyone's hand before sitting down in the front row. I recognized that smile and those eyes. His dirty blond hair was much shorter, making his eyes stand out even more. From a distance, I noticed his pierced ears, which weren't pierced the last time I saw him. He was even better looking now at thirty. He accepted condolences, graciously thanking everyone. Unlike me, he was a people person.

At the end of the ceremony, I hung around, impatiently waiting for my turn to talk to him and shake his hand like all the rest. As time wore on, I grew more and more anxious, my heart beating out of my chest. How could he not see me standing there?

"Terry," I said, attempting to get his attention. "Terry, hello?"

At the sound of my voice, his body froze. With hesitation, he stepped away from everyone and faced me. We just stood there, staring into each other's eyes, at a loss for words. It was him. It was really him. I didn't know what to say or do.

"Scott," he said with a warm, inviting smile, color drained from his face.

"Hi," I said, nervously wringing my fingers. "I'm sorry about your dad. If you don't mind me asking, what happened?"

"He had a heart attack. Heart disease runs in the family."

"Oh, I'm sorry. He was a good guy."

"Yeah." He swallowed hard, looking down and away. To lighten the mood, I changed the subject.

"Your hair's so short, and your ears are pierced. I like it."

His cheeks turned pink. My feelings for him never died, something I always knew, something I feared.

"You look good, too," he said.

I just wanted to hug him and kiss him and take him somewhere away from here. "So… " I sighed, running my fingers through my hair. My eyes wandered, contemplating what to say next. I didn't want to say hi and bye. "You want to—" I figured a few drinks were in order, but he didn't wait for me to finish my question.

"I'd love to," he cut me off.

"You don't even know what I was going to say," I laughed.

"I don't care. Just get me outta here."

Terry and I weaved in and out of the crowd, heading to my car. He sat quietly in the passenger's seat as I drove to a pub on the outskirts of town. More nervous than I'd been in a long time, I had a hard time pretending I wasn't attracted to him.

But he blew it. We could never go back.

Terry fidgeted with his fingers as I ordered two beers at the bar. "Thanks," he said, taking the beer from me as I sat down in the booth across from him. "Wow, this is crazy, huh? Me and you here after all these years. I thought about looking you up, but… well, it doesn't matter. How've you been? What have you been up to?"

"I work with my dad."

"Advertising?" From the bowl in the center of the table, he spooned a handful of popcorn into his palm.

"I'm a graphic designer," I said, but I wasn't in the mood to talk about my job. "How was the Peace Corps?"

"It was an experience. I went to El Salvador."

"Cool. Can you speak Spanish now?" Small talk was painful when all I wanted to do was shout, *"Why the hell didn't you write me, asshole?"*

"Yeah, which has come in handy. When I got home from El Salvador, I applied for a grant to start a camp for inner-city kids. At first I just started with a few kids and two counselors—me and a friend from college. This summer I have about twenty kids per session and four counselors, not including me and Angie. Right now we have a total of four sessions. Next year I hope for six sessions to give even more kids a chance. It's all free, too, scholarship-based, which is the coolest part." Terry was obviously very proud and passionate about his project and accomplishment. "A lot of my campers speak Spanish."

"The camp's at the Lachance Inn and Cottages?" I asked.

"Yeah, but it's still open to the public, too. Business is good."

"I'm glad to hear it. How's your mother?"

Terry paused, looking away from me as he brought the pint of beer to his lips. "Not great. She's had memory problems for a while, but she fell apart after Dad died. She's five years older than him, but I guess she's still kinda young to be diagnosed with Alzheimer's disease. Have you heard of it?"

"Yes."

His eyes filled with water. "I didn't want to do it, but I had to. I couldn't take care of her and run the business and do what I had to do. I mean, I want a life, too, and she always told me she didn't want me to sacrifice my life for her."

"Where is she now?"

"She's at a nursing home. I visit her almost every day."

"I'm sure she's proud of you and your accomplishments. It sounds impressive to me."

Terry looked away, staring out the window.

"I'm sorry," I said, annoyed at myself for upsetting him.

"It's okay. It's really good to see you. I don't see a ring. You're not married yet?"

"No." I decided now was the perfect time to order more beer. I got up and bought two more, returning to our booth. "No, I'm not married yet, but Aimee hopes we'll be married soon."

"Aimee," Terry laughed. "I knew you'd get a girl."

"Stop laughing." I tossed a few pieces of popcorn at him. "She expects me to ask her to marry me. I don't know what to do."

"You know what to do, especially if you're having doubts, and it sounds like you are."

"She's really nice. She's a lawyer with the ACLU. I think you'd like her."

"I probably would." He stifled a few more chuckles. "How long have you been with her?"

"Two years."

"That's a long time. It's probably about time you got married. You're not getting any younger. Pretty soon you'll be thirty, then forty, and then..."

Annoyed with Terry's sarcasm, I didn't want to hear anymore and got up, ready to leave. He was toying with me. I should have stayed home.

"Hey!" Terry shouted to me as I headed to the door. "Wait up. I need a ride back to my hotel. Hey, Scottie, don't just leave me here. I'm sorry for laughing."

"No, you're not," I said. I didn't blame him for laughing, and I wasn't ready to say goodbye to him.

"Yes, I am." He got up from the booth. "Will you at least drive me to my hotel? I promise not to laugh anymore."

But I liked his laugh.

"Fine," I said. "Come on."

Neither of us were ready to say goodbye. As we sat at the hotel bar, I listened to Terry tell me all about El Salvador and how he was a teacher in a tiny village. After a few more beers, we decided to have dinner together, sharing a bottle of wine. We were both feeling pretty good, enjoying each other's company, freely laughing and chatting about everything and anything that came to mind. I couldn't do that with anyone else.

Terry strategically rested his foot against mine under the table. As he rubbed his foot against my ankle, warmth soared through my veins, causing me to shift in my seat. Terry smiled in a way that told me he knew what he was doing. I didn't say or do anything to stop him.

After dinner, Terry ordered a round of tequila shots. At this rate, I was on the verge of getting so drunk I wouldn't be able to drive home. I'd been drinking since two o'clock.

"Are you going to make me drink both of them?" he asked, referring to the two shots on the table. "Okay, here it goes," he said and downed them. I got up and ordered more shots at the bar. I sat beside him instead of across from him. "You wanna lick the salt off my palm like you did ten years ago?"

"Ha-ha," I said, although tempted. I shook the salt on top of my hand before chugging down a shot of tequila. "I think this is a ploy to get me good and drunk."

"You're a fun drunk," he said as I sucked a lime. "And you're already drunk."

"But I have to drive."

"You're not driving anywhere."

Within minutes, Terry had consumed three shots. His hand landed on my knee, contemplating another round of tequila. Instead of getting up to go to the bar, he called the waitress over and ordered two more.

When Terry tried to get up to go to the bathroom, he nearly tumbled over. "Whoa," I said, catching him before he fell. "Let's go."

"Where are we going?"

"To your room."

Draping his arm over my shoulder, I led him out of the hotel restaurant. Once we made it to his room, he giggled as his hand wavered back and forth, attempting to unlock the door. I took the key from him and unlocked the door myself.

"I have to pee so bad," he said, stumbling to the bathroom. He left the door open, relieving himself over the toilet. On his way out of the bathroom, he stripped down to his underwear, collapsing on the only bed in the room. He laughed at himself, staggering to his feet. "You can't drive. You've had too much to drink, too."

He was right.

I froze as he pulled my tie loose. "You're drunk," I reminded him, on the brink of attacking him.

"Come to bed."

I swatted his hand away as he attempted to unbutton my shirt.

"That's right. You're not gay," he said. "I'll just ignore your boner, and you can stop looking at mine."

"You're too drunk to get it up."

"I'm so offended."

As he was about to take out his dick, I grabbed his hand to stop him. He drunkenly fell into my arms. I wanted him in the worst way. As we hugged, I breathed in his scent, my lips against his neck. His body went limp and heavy. That's when I realized he had passed out. I helped him into bed and brought the covers over his half-naked body.

I undressed down to my boxers and got in bed beside him. In Terry's drunken slumber, he draped an arm over my chest. I remained awake, watching this sleeping beauty. There was no one else like him, and there never would be.

Eventually I dozed off, sleeping until the sun shone through the curtains. At ten in the morning, Terry was still asleep, lying on his stomach, his back moving up and down subtly. It was time for me to leave as much as I didn't want to.

"Hey, Terry," I said, placing a hand on his bare shoulder. He didn't stir until I slid my hand all the way down the middle of his back. "I have to go," I whispered, patting his back. "Terry," I raised my voice. "I have to get going."

Yawning and stretching his arms, he rolled over to face me. "Huh?" he said, his eyes still closed.

My heart stopped, and all I thought about was kissing him. I didn't want to leave. "I have to go."

His eyes sprung open. There was a sadness in them that I hadn't seen since he talked about his mother the day before. "Can I call you?"

"Yes, I'd love to hear from you."

"And if you're ever in Vermont, feel free to stop by. I'll take you water skiing... or maybe go to a drive-in or... or... maybe swing from a rope."

I liked all of his suggestions.

"Call me when you get home," I said. "So I know you got home safe. It's a long ride and you're hung over."

"You were always such a worrier."

"Just call me, okay?" I said, squeezing his shoulder.

"Yes, I'll call you."

"I'll talk to you soon." I almost kissed him goodbye, but I got up before I had the chance to succumb to temptation.

As I headed out of the room, I felt Terry's eyes on me. I didn't look back as I left.

19

Chapter 19

Terry

My body yearned for him, my love for him as strong as it was ten years ago. I rolled over, taking a deep breath into the sheets where Scott had slept all night. The sheets still smelled of him, his scent lingering in the bed and room.

When I accepted the invitation to the Memorial Day ceremony, I had hoped to run into Scott. I wanted answers. We promised to write to each other, but Scott broke his promise to live a lie. People expected him to marry a woman and have children with a house in the suburbs. If he did what people expected of him, he'd sacrifice his life, trapped in a heterosexual marriage. I felt sorry for him. I didn't ask Scott any questions because I didn't want to hear the answers. He wanted me as much as I wanted him, but he didn't bite. He came close, though.

Ray Lawrence was no Scott Prescott. I met Ray, a forty-seven-year-old English teacher, while volunteering at a hospice house for AIDS patients. Two months before we met, Ray lost his partner of ten years to alcoholism. We used each other to fill the voids in our lives. For me, only one person could fill that void.

Ray and I found comfort in each other's arms. This relationship wouldn't amount to anything, but it served a purpose... until now. Scott and I still shared a connection, and I hoped—more than anything—that I'd see him again, that he'd take me up on my offer and come to Vermont.

I needed hope right now. The sudden death of my dad hit me hard. Putting my mother in a nursing home just made matters worse. It was the hardest decision I ever had to make.

Ray wasn't one for talking or listening. Our pseudo relationship was all about sex. I could talk to Scott and he listened. Within minutes of returning home, I picked up the phone to let him know I got "home safely." At thirty years old, I was more than capable of taking care of myself, but he worried about me? I had a hunch that he just wanted me to call him. And to be honest, I couldn't wait to call him, to hear his voice again so soon after we said goodbye. Disappointed he wasn't home, I left a message on his answering machine.

"Hi, Scott, it's Terry," I started. "I just wanted to let you know I'm home. Call me when you get a chance. It was good seeing you. Bye." There was so much more I wanted to say. A half an hour later, Scott returned my call. I picked up after the first ring.

"Terry?"

My hand shook as I held the receiver to my ear. "Yeah, hi," I said. "I just wanted to let you know I got home safely."

"Good. I'm glad you called to let me know. You know me, I worry about everything."

Warm chills ran up and down my spine as I remembered his hand on my back and shoulder in the hotel room. I wanted to reach through the phone and touch him. Every part of me wanted him in the worst way.

Ray showed up at the right time. We hadn't been together in almost a week, and I wasn't in the mood to be alone, looking forward to relieving my sexual frustration. At six feet four and two hundred and twenty solid pounds, Ray was a big-time college football star in his younger years.

Scott mentioned he had a girlfriend named Aimee, someone he said I'd "like," something I had a hard time stomaching when he said it. At least he wasn't engaged, and I hoped it'd stay that way. Besides that brief mention, he avoided talking about their relationship. In fact, he talked very little of the past ten years. Over the next twenty minutes, Scott did most of the listening while I did most of the talking. As I talked, imagining him nodding and smiling on the other end, Ray squeezed my shoulder on his way to the bedroom.

"I have to go," I finally said to Scott. I didn't want to keep Ray waiting, eager to do something with this killer boner of mine.

"Okay," Scott said with a quiet sigh. "It was really good talking to you."

"Yeah, it was good talking to you, too."

Before hanging up, we promised we'd talk again. I certainly hoped so.

Naked in my bed, Ray lay on top of the covers, his legs stretched out in front of him, his ankles crossed. I shed my clothes and pounced on top of him. "Whoa," he said. "I've never seen you like this."

"Just shut up and fuck me," I said.

"Wow." Ray flipped me on my stomach. "What's gotten into you, huh? I like it." He propped me up on my hands and knees and did exactly what I told him to do. No matter how hard I pretended, I couldn't pretend Scott was the one inside me. Unlike Scott, Ray never let me top him. Tonight I asked Ray again and he said no. "You know I don't do that."

I stormed into the bathroom, slamming the door shut. I finished myself off over the toilet, imagining Scott watching me.

"Hey, don't be like that," Ray said behind the bathroom door. "You can be such a little bitch, you know that?" He'd called me that before, along with princess and prima donna. “Who were you talking to on the phone?”

I didn’t answer as I looked down at my sticky hand, my body trembling as I thought of Scott.

“It was him, wasn’t it? It was Scott.”

“Yeah, it was him.” I had mentioned Scott a hundred times over the years. After washing my hands, I found Ray putting his clothes back on when I returned to the bedroom,

“I hope you see him again,” he said.

So did I.

But Scott reneged on his promise and the next phone call never came. What was I thinking, anyway? I expected too much. I was like some naïve, lovesick teenager and all alone with no one to talk to. Ray wasn’t one for talking. My business partner, Angie Kapinsky, was a good friend and a great business partner and I owed a lot to her, but I couldn’t talk to her, either. She would have just told me to forget him or move on, or that he’s “not worth it.” To me, he was worth it. I wanted him back even though I wrote to him all the time for two years and he never once wrote back. Time healed all wounds, right? Forgive and forget?

* * *

Jodie Moreau, a former camp counselor, now worked as a full-time staff at the Inn and Cottages. A social butterfly, she enjoyed manning the front desk, checking the guests in and out, meeting new people every day. There was also Philip Silva, a retired social studies teacher who helped out. He didn’t mind gardening, my least favorite chore. In fact, many teachers worked at the Inn during the summer. I was fortunate I had plenty of help and worked with some great people. I promised my parents I’d keep the place running as long as possible, hopefully forever.

"Hey, Terry," Jodie said, standing in the doorway of the office that once belonged to my parents. It was a complete mess and totally disorganized. I hadn't had time to go through the filing cabinets and stacks of papers.

"Yeah?" I replied, not looking up from my notebook, trying to focus on putting together the counselors' assignments for the upcoming session.

"Someone's here to see you. He specifically asked for you and it's not Ray."

"Did he say who he was?" I asked.

"No, but he's really cute."

Cute? Smiling, I turned around to look at my twenty-two-year-old receptionist. "Does he have dark brown hair and brown eyes, kinda tall?"

"Yeah."

Giddy with excitement at the possibility of who was waiting for me in the lobby, I dropped my pen and pushed past her. Scott stood in the lobby, a duffel bag at his feet, dressed as I remembered him all those years ago: a tan t-shirt and forest green shorts and sandals, not in the stuffy suit and tie with a white button-down shirt that he wore to the Memorial Day event.

"Hi," he said. "Sorry I didn't call."

We hadn't spoken in three days, not since I got home. Since that day, I bet he'd been contemplating coming here, driving himself crazy, wondering if he should go or not.

"Do you have a room available?" he asked.

"Um... uh... yeah," I said, strangely nervous and in awe of his presence. He seemed as nervous as I was, shoving his hands inside the pockets of his shorts. "How long do you need the room for?"

"Three nights and four days. I told my dad I'd be back next Monday. He's pissed I'm taking almost a week off even though I told him I needed a break."

"I'll even give you a discount," I teased him as I looked at the calendar to see what rooms and cottages were available. It was still early in the season, so there was plenty of availability. The first camp session wasn't for another three weeks. "Would you like a cottage?"

"Yeah, sure."

"Cool. Let's go."

Scott picked up his bag and followed me to the cottages. I moved out of my old cottage years ago. For old time's sake, I would have taken him to that one, but it was booked. I took him to the next closest one.

"Where are all the kids?" he asked.

"They're coming in three weeks," I said. "It's quiet here right now."

Scott's eyes wandered around the room, examining it. He dropped his duffel bag on the floor. He looked good. Damn good. His late twenties suited him. His shoulders were slightly broader, his arms and calves more muscular. I was mostly unchanged, just as skinny, my hair shorter.

"Is it okay?" I asked.

"It's great," he answered, his voice shaking, both nervous and excited. "Are you hungry? I'm starving. Are you busy now?"

I had a lot of work to do, but work could wait. "No," I lied.

"Okay," he smiled. "Let me take a quick shower, and we'll grab something to eat."

"Yeah, sure. I'll meet you in the restaurant."

I stood there stupidly, watching him enter the bathroom, wishing I was going with him. He glanced over his shoulder, smiling before closing the door. After regathering my senses, I ran back to my place, took a quick shower, then went to the restaurant. I ran a skeleton crew in the kitchen this early in the season, so only the sous chef, Carlos, was there at one in the afternoon. Searching the fridge, I found the veggie burgers I made the day before. Before assuming he'd eat them, I decided to hold off and ask him what he wanted.

"Nothing's changed," Scott said, startling me in the kitchen doorway while I sifted through the fridge. "I'm sorry. I shouldn't be in here. I'll leave."

"No, it's okay. I can throw some burgers on the grill. Well, a veggie burger for me."

"Did you make them?" he asked, standing beside me, peering inside the fridge. Goosebumps prickled my arms as his arm brushed against mine.

"Yes, this morning."

"I'll have one of those."

While I grilled, Scott waded along the bank of the lake, his hands in the pockets of his shorts. I felt like no time had passed. "The water's still kind of cold this time of year, huh?" he said. "But cold water never bothered me. Maybe you could take me water skiing later."

"I'd love to," I said.

"I haven't skied in years. I hope I can still get up."

"I'm sure you can."

With the cooked burgers, Scott and I sat on the grass, the lake only a few feet away. One boat floated in the middle of the lake, a father and son fishing.

"I always liked it here," he said. "It's nice and quiet... peaceful."

"You won't think it's so peaceful in a couple of weeks."

"It's a good thing I'll be gone by then, huh? So... do you still sing and play?"

"Yes. Maybe I'll play for you some time."

Scott's cheeks turned pink, nodding and smiling.

As promised, I took Scott out on the lake. For someone who supposedly didn't mind the cold water, he hesitated before getting in. When he was eighteen, he had no trouble getting up on skis, but today he had a hard time and floundered, shrieking each time he fell.

"I thought the cold water didn't bother you," I laughed while he swam in the water, searching for the skis that slipped off him when he fell. I hadn't laughed so hard and so naturally in a long time.

After an hour of swimming, we lounged on the boat, soaking up the late afternoon sun. For early June, it was warmer than usual, but as the sun went down, the air grew chilly. Scott wrapped a towel around his body like a cocoon and closed his eyes. He looked like he needed sleep, like he desperately needed this mini-vacation.

I had a lot of questions I wanted to ask him and couldn't bite my tongue any longer. "Are you going to marry her?" I asked.

"Who?" he yawned.

"Aimee."

"No."

"Then why are you with her? And why are you with a girl, anyway?"

"Do you want to marry everyone you go out with?" he shot back at me.

"No, but you've been with her for two years."

"I don't want to talk about this."

Unlike Scott, I was wide awake and full of questions, dying for answers. "Do you like women now, or are you still gay?" I prodded. "Or are you bisexual, or just sexually confused?"

"Fuck," he sighed, sitting up. "I'm trying to relax here, and you're making it impossible. Let's go back so I can get some rest."

"Fine," I said, hopping in the driver's seat of the boat. I shouldn't have said anything, but my mouth sometimes had a mind of its own. We returned to land in awkward silence. Scott jumped out of the boat before I docked it. "I'm sorry," I said. "I didn't mean to pry. I'm just curious."

Scott headed back to his cottage as I trailed behind him, admiring his backside. "Be ready in twenty minutes," he said, not turning around to look at me. "We're going out to eat."

As Scott closed the door in my face, I stood there confused, wondering more than ever why he wasted his time with Aimee these past two years. He wasn't straight, bisexual, or sexually confused; he was scared.

20

Chapter 20

Terry

After my drunken, humiliating event last weekend, I stayed away from alcohol tonight. Scott and I went to a local pizza joint where Scott gorged on pizza and beer, followed by ice cream at the same place I took him and his kid brother ten years ago. I was a frequent customer there. Scott was often quiet, letting me do most of the talking. He often appeared lost in thought. In awkward silence, we licked our ice cream cones as we passed the downtown shops that had just closed for the evening.

"I want a family," Scott finally said. "That's why I'm with Aimee."

"I want a family, too," I said, "but that doesn't mean I'm going to find a girl to marry."

"Then how do you suppose you'll have a family?"

"There's gotta be some unwanted kids out there in desperate need of a home that the state's willing to give to a single gay guy or gay couple if I ever settle down with someone. I know it's not the same as having your own kid, but I don't see any other way. It's not like I'm going to have sex with a woman just so I can have a kid. That's selfish, don't you think?"

Scott said nothing as we continued to walk, but I couldn't keep my mouth shut.

"I guess you have your parents to deal with," I said. "At least you have parents. I saw my mother last week and she had no idea who I was. What do you think about two guys adopting kids? Do you think it's feasible, or do you think it's wrong?"

Scott was silent while I continued.

"Do you think you could spend the rest of your life with a woman you don't love just for the sake of having a family?"

"Who says I don't love her?"

"I guess I'm being judgmental and presumptuous again," I said. "So you don't have sex with any men?"

"I'm happy with the way things are." If he was happy with the way things were, I doubted he'd be here with me right now. "Imagine the poor kids being raised by a couple of fags. School alone would be hell."

"You don't know that. If you raise them right and make sure they have a good head on their shoulders, they should be okay."

"You were always such an optimist. Ready to change the world."

"I wouldn't say that. Don't you think gay couples should have the same opportunities as straight couples?"

He didn't answer. Sometimes Scott could be hard to read. I didn't know what his silence meant.

"Do you think you deserve to be punished because you're gay?"

"Who says I'm gay?" he responded.

I tried not to laugh. "Whatever you say. You came on to me first, remember?"

"It was a long time ago."

"Yeah," was all I said and decided to drop the subject.

Avoiding any more touchy subjects, we hit the drive-in. In my dad's old pickup, the two of us lay in the truck's bed, watching *Indiana Jones and the Last Crusade*. I so wanted to rest my head on Scott's shoulder like I used to do, but I controlled myself. I wanted Scott to make the first move.

Halfway through the movie, Scott scooted closer to me so our bodies touched, his arm against mine as we lay stretched out in the truck. He traced my fingers and knuckles. Dizzy at his touch, I took a deep breath, trying to regain my senses. His eyes remained focused on the big screen, his fingers focused on mine. I thought he was going to slip his hand in mine, but he didn't. Instead, he swallowed hard, pulling his hand away, folding his hands in his lap.

"Scott," I said. He instantly bolted upright.

"I need more popcorn," he said. "Do you want anything?"

"No, thanks."

Scott and I had the same goals in life. Because of this, I hoped we could make it work, but then I remembered what my mother said: was Scott Prescott strong enough for a lifelong homosexual relationship?

Maybe.

* * *

Scott and I met up for breakfast in the morning and then again later in the day for a swim. I had work to do, so I couldn't entertain him all day, although I thought about him all afternoon, making my work meaningless.

At two thirty, I gave up on work and searched the grounds for Scott. I found him in his swimsuit, lying on his stomach in the grass, reading a book. I fought the temptation to run my hands all the way down his bare back and over his perfect ass. As I cast a shadow over his book, he closed it and rolled onto his back, looking up at me.

"Hey," he said, squinting, the sun blinding him. "I thought you had work to do."

"I'm not in the mood to work," I said, taking off my shirt. His cheeks reddened, his eyes wandering down my body. He was as turned on as I was. "Come with me."

Like old times, I took him for a ride in the rowboat to our secret spot. I hadn't been out here in a long time. Scott turned around as I took off my swimsuit and tossed it in the boat.

"We're too old for this," he said as I approached the rope.

"Who says I'm old? And you're not even thirty." I swung from the rope, letting go above the cold water. Minutes later, Scott nearly fell on top of me.

"Fuck, it's freezing!" he shrieked.

I couldn't stop laughing. Annoyed with my laughter, Scott splashed me over and over, but his splashes made me laugh harder. My laughter subsided as he stood behind me, wrapping his arms around me. He breathed heavily against my neck. In the cold water, my body was burning up.

"I want to take you out to dinner," he said. He kissed my neck and broke away from me. "I'm hungry. Let's go."

I wasn't ready to go, but there was no talking Scott into staying. He got dressed and waited for me in the boat, claiming he was "starving." He was always "starving."

We ate at a small Italian restaurant downtown. Over a bottle of wine, we talked about everything and anything, staying away from such hot topics as girlfriends. It was safer to talk about Ronald Reagan and George Bush and our equal disgust with them.

I had promised to sing and play for Scott, so tonight we went to the pub instead of saying goodnight to each other. On a Thursday night, the pub was empty. I sat on my usual stool while Scott sat a few feet away. He sipped his pint of beer, keeping his eyes on me the whole time. All I wanted to do was hop off the stool, tear off his clothes, and do him right on top of the table. He looked at me the same way, but something was holding him back. Something was gnawing at him inside, but he wouldn't say what it was.

As I played *The Boxer*, I watched Scott rummage through the bar, finding what he was looking for. He sat back down with a bottle of tequila, two shot glasses, salt, and two limes he found in the mini refrigerator under the bar. As the song came to a close, he had already had three shots. I had a feeling he was drinking to distract himself, more so tonight than ever before.

"Come join me," he said.

Taking him up on his offer, I sat down beside him. He handed me a shot, which I chugged, but I promised myself I wouldn't get drunk. Before downing another shot, he shook some salt on my palm and licked it all off.

"I usually don't drink this much, you know," he said. "Only when I'm on vacation."

"You don't have to explain anything to me," I said.

With one hand, he fingered my ear lobes, circling my gold studs. With his other hand, he poured shot after shot. While getting good and drunk, he flirted with me, coming on to me. "I love your earrings," he said. "You'd look good with diamonds... or onyx."

"Onyx?" I laughed.

"Yeah. The black would really make your blue eyes stand out. I always liked your eyes." After the last shot, he stood up, only to plop back down in his seat. "I should go to bed. I've had too much to drink... again. I feel like such a drunk."

"Come on, I'll help you."

"I don't need your help." He successfully stood up this time. "I'm okay."

Hesitantly, I walked toward the door, assuming Scott was behind me, but he hadn't budged, standing at the table.

"Why the fuck didn't you write me!" His voice quivered with rage.

"I wrote you all the time and you didn't write me back. Why? Why, Terry?"

Taken aback, I turned around to face him, more confused than stunned because I had no idea what he was talking about. Without warning, Scott picked up a chair and chucked it across the room, aiming for my head. "You fucking asshole!" he spat at me.

As he went to pick up another chair, I lost my cool and charged toward him. Shoving him, I pinned him against the bar. "What the hell's wrong with you?" I said, gripping his wrists, overpowering Scott for once in my life.

"Let go of me, asshole," he said through gritted teeth.

"I wrote to you for two years straight. I even sent you postcards from El Salvador. You didn't write to me because you thought I didn't write to you, is that it?"

"No, that's not it. I wrote to you all the time."

As his demeanor softened, his anger dissipating, my grip loosened. "Well, I never received any letters," I said. "Why would my parents keep them from me? It doesn't make sense."

"I don't know. Maybe my dad did something. Maybe he threatened your parents. You swear you wrote to me?"

"Yes, all the time," I said, tracing the outline of his scratchy jaw with my finger. "I'd never lie to you. What about your parents? Do you think they did something with your mail? They must have, right?"

Scott paused before responding. "I feel so stupid," he mumbled, looking down and away. "I never got any mail in college and I was too stupid to question it. I'm so fucking stupid."

"I understand why your parents would do it, but I don't understand why my parents would, even if your dad threatened mine. I'd ask my mother if she knew anything about it, but she wouldn't be able to tell me."

With his head tilted down, Scott sniffed.

"Please don't cry," I said, squeezing his shoulder. "It's not too late for us, is it?"

"I hope it's not too late," he whispered, looking up, a film of water coating his eyes.

"No, it's not too late."

With his eyes fixed with mine, Scott placed his hand on the back of my neck and kissed my mouth. I inhaled, returning his kiss. Exhaling, I moaned into his mouth, kissing him harder and longer. There was no stopping Scott. As we kissed hungrily and desperately, he tore off his clothes. He had been suppressing his sexuality far too long.

"You really should play hard to get," I laughed as he kicked off his shorts and boxers.

"I'm going to fucking kill my parents," he said, undoing my jeans. "I never stopped thinking about you." He shoved his hand inside the front of my underwear, groping me.

"Maybe we should go to my house and..." My voice trailed off as Scott kissed my chest, making his way to my stomach. On his knees, he yanked my jeans and underwear down to my ankles and sucked my cock harder than anyone had ever sucked.

Scott moved so fast I didn't have time to respond. He pushed me on the table and pulled my jeans and underwear all the way off. If it was someone other than Scott, I would have resisted, but we had waited far too long. I let him take me right there on the table. Grunting against my neck, he thrust hard inside me—maybe too hard. In response to the intense pain, I accidentally bit his neck.

"I'm sorry," he said as his cock throbbed inside me. "Did I hurt you?"

"I'll be okay."

"I haven't been with a man in a long time. You feel so good."

I held him to me as he cried against my neck, his body trembling.

"It's okay," I said in his ear. "Hey... hey, Scott, look at me."

Reluctantly, he looked at me, his eyes red and puffy.

"It's going to be okay," I reassured him. "No one's ever fucked me on a table before."

"I don't have AIDS. I promise you I'm clean. I'm sorry, Terry. I... I just... I couldn't help myself. I'm sorry."

He burst into tears. Nothing was worse than seeing a grown man cry, especially Scott.

"Don't cry," I said, hugging him. "Everything's cool." My body shuddered as he pulled out of me.

"Sorry." He rubbed his eyes.

"Let's get out of here and go to my house. You can fuck me all night if you want."

"Yeah, okay," he said, regaining his composure. "I'd like that."

"And maybe you'll let me fuck you."

"I'd like that, too."

"But before we go to my house, I need to do something." I hoped to get to the bottom of these missing letters. What really happened?

Back to his normal self, Scott moaned about his grumbling stomach and didn't want to stop at my office that was once my dad's. I was determined to find those letters.

"What makes you think your parents saved my letters?" Scott asked as I tore through the office.

"I just have this feeling," I said, dumping the contents of my dad's desk drawers on the floor. All I found were outstanding bills. "Hmm... I guess I have some bills to pay. Don't just stand there, Scottie. Help me."

Scott opened up the jam-packed filing cabinet, pulling so hard that the whole thing came out, tumbling to the floor. "Your dad wasn't very organized, was he?" he said.

In the back of the last filing cabinet, I found an overstuffed manila folder jammed all the way in the back. I discovered envelope after envelope, letters all from Scott. On top of the stack was a handwritten note from my father.

Dear Terry,

If you're finding these letters, it means I'm either dead and gone, or you've found Scott again or maybe Scott has found you. I wish I could explain why I did what I did, but I'm too ashamed to admit the reasons why. I saved the letters for you because I wanted you to know how much Scott loved you. I hope you find happiness. You deserve it. I hope you'll be able to forgive me someday.

Love, Dad.

Nothing he wrote made sense to me. I couldn't picture my dad doing anything wrong, at least so egregious he nearly ruined my life. It wasn't in his character to do something so vindictive. There must have been at least a hundred letters in the folder.

"What's he talking about?" Scott asked after reading my dad's chicken scratch.

"I have no idea," I said. "Do you know something I don't?"

"If I did, I'd tell you. My dad must have dirt on Frankie or something."

"I don't know," I sighed, heading out of the office with the folder. "My dad was a good guy. I can't believe it."

Maybe I didn't know my dad as well as I thought I did. He sounded like he had some dark secret that no one knew about... except for maybe Tommy Lachance.

21

Chapter 21

Scott

Tucked away on the far left side of the inn, Terry grew up in a semi-detached, quaint house I didn't know existed.

"Make yourself at home," he said, tossing the folder of unopened letters on the small kitchen table. He intended to read them, even though I warned him that some of them weren't so nice.

Dying for food, I opened the refrigerator. There was a carton of orange juice, a half gallon of milk, a six-pack of beer, and boxes of Hostess Cupcakes, Ding-Dongs, and Twinkies. I never pictured Terry as a junk food fiend. "What's this?" I asked, referring to all the junk food. "You call this food?"

More focused on my letters, he didn't respond until I shoved a Twinkie in his mouth.

"Don't read those," I said. "Let's go to your room."

With the box of Twinkies, I followed Terry up the stairs. At the far end of the hallway was one bedroom, which I presumed to be the master bedroom next to a hardly used guest bedroom. Farther down the hall was Terry's room. An acoustic guitar leaned against his unmade bed.

A laundry basket of clean clothes sat at the foot of the bed. To the side of the window was a painting I did years ago, a painting Terry always liked, the one with the toddlers playing by the lake. I never painted for pleasure anymore. After finishing my Twinkie, I opened another.

"I can't believe you still have this," I said.

"It's one of my favorites," he said.

In awe of his presence, as if I hadn't just fucked him raw in the pub, I watched him drop the folder on his nightstand before taking off his shirt.

"It's my turn," he said, stepping into me as he undid his jeans. "I haven't been inside a guy in a long time. Will you let me?"

I nodded, swallowing my last bite of Twinkie.

"There's no rush," he said, lifting my shirt over my head. "We have all night and morning, or maybe a lifetime."

In each other's arms, we collapsed onto his bed. I welcomed him inside me. Filling me completely, all the way up there, my lips clamped down on his neck. With his hand around my cock, he thrust hard.

"Ssh, it's okay," he said as I cried out against his shoulder. "I'm here, Scott. I'm not going anywhere."

Terry kissed me all over my face, kissing away my tears. Minutes after finishing round one, I rolled him onto his back, ready for round two.

Exhausted, yet content and sexually satisfied, I rested my head against his chest. He pulled out a letter from the folder. "Oh, no," I said. "Don't read them in front of me."

Smirking, he tore open the envelope despite my plea. "Uh-oh," he said. "This one's not very nice. *Why the fuck haven't you written me, you lying piece of shit?*"

I yanked the letter out of his hands and ripped it to shreds. "Read them when I'm not around, okay?"

"Fine. I'll read them after you leave on Sunday."

I didn't want to think about Sunday.

"Or you could just stay here," he said. "Give me one good reason why you can't stay."

"J-O-B," I said.

"You don't need it. You told me you never wanted to work for your dad, working sixty to eighty hours a week. It wouldn't be like that here. You could get a job in Burlington. It's only an hour away."

"I'm not prepared to have this conversation. I've only been here for two days."

"So? I feel like we've picked up where we left off. That's gotta mean something, right?"

I knew he was right but needed time at home to sort things out, a girlfriend being one of them.

"I don't want to wait another ten years to see you," he said.

As Terry looked away, I placed a hand on his bare, knobby knee. A few stray tears fell down his cheeks. "That won't happen," I said. "I promise you."

"I don't have anyone." He stared at the wall. "My dad dropped dead. He was outside mowing the lawn on our sit-down mower, and he had a heart attack and died just like that. With you, I feel connected to someone again. I can't lose anyone else."

I hugged him and kissed his cheek. "I feel at home with you. You'll always have me."

Terry bawled his eyes out against my shoulder. This wasn't entirely about me. He had no one to share his grief with over the death of his father and his mother's progressive illness. "I'm so sorry for your loss, but I'm here now," I said as he sobbed in my arms. "I'll always be there for you."

"Promise?" He pulled away from me.

I never, ever wanted Terry to feel alone again. He was way too good of a person, the most selfless, giving man I'd ever met in my life. I intended to keep my promises.

* * *

Disappointed to wake to a cold, empty bed, I threw on Terry's bathrobe and followed the intoxicating aroma of fresh, brewing coffee. In the kitchen doorway, I stopped, staring dumbfounded at the sight before me. At the kitchen sink stood a big, tall, and somewhat menacing man, washing the stack of dirty dishes in the sink. From the looks of it, Terry hadn't done the dishes in at least a week. I didn't want to move, afraid this man would do something to me. I was six feet, around a hundred and seventy-five pounds, while this man was at least six foot four or five and two hundred and fifty pounds. Terry was slightly shorter than I was and barely a hundred and fifty pounds. Dark-haired and thinning on top with bulging, protruding muscles, he looked like a bodybuilder or retired NFL player.

Last night Terry told me he "had no one," so I had no reason to believe he had a boyfriend. I always pictured Terry with someone like me and not this bodybuilder who was strangely comfortable in Terry's kitchen.

"Oh, you must be Scott," the man said, wiping his hands on a dish towel as he approached me. I instinctively backed away due to the pure size of this man. "Terry's told me so much about you." This man shook my hand exuberantly with such enthusiasm I thought I was in the Twilight Zone.

Where the hell's Terry? I wondered, shaking this unknown man's hand. I thought he'd never let go.

"I was on my way to work and thought I'd stop by," he said. "Want some coffee?"

"Um... uh... sure," I said.

As I stood there, thinking of ways to escape, he returned to the kitchen counter and poured a cup of coffee. "You're younger than I thought you'd be. How old are you? Twenty-five, twenty-six?"

"Twenty-seven," I said.

"I was close. You look nice in Terry's bathrobe."

"I'm sorry," I finally said, continuing to stand there awkwardly. "Who are you?"

"Oh, I'm Ray, a friend of Terry's. Sit down. You're making me nervous standing there."

"A friend?" I said suspiciously. He seemed way too comfortable in his house to be just "a friend."

He shrugged. "Yeah, you could say that. Terry's a young, good looking guy. He's hard to resist."

If he said he was hard to resist, then my suspicions were correct: Ray was Terry's boyfriend.

"He's got a good heart, too," Ray added, "and it only belongs to one person and he's standing right there." He pointed his finger at me, walking back to me with that fresh cup of coffee I desperately needed. "Now sit your ass down." Afraid of the repercussions, I did what he said.

"So you're not his—" I was going to say boyfriend, but he answered the question before I finished asking it.

"No. We just use each other for the same thing."

Sex, I concluded. That was the saddest thing I'd ever heard.

The screen door squeaked open and slammed shut. Terry entered, carrying a bag of groceries. "Ray, what are you doing here?" Terry asked, glancing uneasily at me.

"I was on my way to work and thought I'd check on you to see how you're doing. I can see you're doing just fine," Ray said, winking at me.

This was really, really awkward.

"Oh, how kind," Terry said with a hint of sarcasm in his voice. "And you're cleaning again. You know it drives me crazy."

"And you know I have OCD," he said, wiping down the counter

vigorously with a sponge.

Terry mouthed "*I'm sorry,*" to me, dropping the bag of groceries on the table.

"Sit down," Ray said to Terry. "I'll make breakfast. What do you have here?" He sifted through the brown paper bag. "Hmm... eggs. At least Terry's not vegan. I'll make scrambled eggs."

Ray made a batch of scrambled eggs and devoured most of them himself, in addition to four pieces of toast and many strips of bacon. Terry specifically bought the bacon for me, but I only got one strip.

Over breakfast, Ray told me all about how he and Terry met as volunteers at a hospice house. He also mentioned his long-time partner who died of cirrhosis at only forty-two. I could see how he and Terry found each other.

"What's gotten into you today?" Terry said to Ray. "You never talk this much."

"I'm in a good mood," Ray said. "It's a beautiful day out, and you're finally smiling."

"Do I look like I'm smiling?" Terry said with a deadpan expression on his face.

"Yes, your eyes are smiling and this one here." He pointed his finger at me again. "He can't wait to get you back upstairs. I bet you boys were fucking like rabbits all night."

"*Fucking like rabbits*?" Terry and I mouthed to each other, giggling under our breath.

"You're not leaving this time, are you?" Ray asked me. "Don't leave him. You boys are crazy about each other."

"He didn't leave by choice the last time," Terry said.

"Yeah, so you told me," Ray said. "Well," he sighed. "I guess I better get going, let you boys get on with it."

Relief swept over Terry's face when he finally left. "I'm so sorry," Terry said, squeezing my knee. "I wasn't expecting him to show up.

Just so you know, he's not a boyfriend. He's a friend with benefits. Are you mad?"

"No," I said. "He just caught me by surprise. I was scared for a few minutes. He could have really kicked my ass."

"He wouldn't hurt anyone." His fingers brushed against my cock that was growing harder and harder by the second. "Let's not talk about him anymore."

I kissed him as he pulled the belt loose, opening my robe. "I'm really scum, you know that?" I said.

"Why do you say that?"

"Because I have a girlfriend. I'm a fucking asshole." Going home and telling her and everyone the truth was going to be a disaster. Aimee planned on spending the rest of her life with me while I had other plans. I dreaded that conversation.

"No, you're not," Terry said. "Fear makes people do crazy things, but I know you'll do the right thing."

"You're always so optimistic." I looked down at his hand on my cock.

"I love you, Scott." He kissed my mouth. "I don't want to let you go."

"That feels so good," I said against his lips as he moved my cock back and forth. "I love you."

"Stay with me."

"I have to go home and sort some shit out," I said, swallowing hard, enjoying his hand on my cock. "As much as I'd just love to pack up and come out here and stay with you."

Terry jerked his hand away, abruptly standing up. He was angry, not a typical emotion for him. "I have this sinking suspicion that if you leave here, you're never coming back," he said.

Haphazardly closing my robe, I went to him. "That won't happen."

Shaking his head, he backed away from me. "What happened to your optimism? Just a minute ago, you told me you think I'll make the right decision."

"Yeah, but I'm realistic, too."

"I won't ever let you go," I said, placing a hand on his shoulder. "You're right; I'm going to make the right decision. I promise I'll come back." I kissed and hugged him. He hugged me back, slipping his hands inside my robe again. "So... you wanna go upstairs and fuck like rabbits?"

* * *

Terry blew off work to spend his time with me before I left on Sunday. We swam, swung from a rope, and fucked our brains out. Not once did I think about my job or my parents.

On Saturday night, we danced to music from the jukebox for hours, dancing to each song as if it was both the first and last dance of our lives. I couldn't remember ever doing this with Aimee. She would have loved it, but I couldn't bring myself to do it; not with her.

As he made breakfast Sunday morning, Terry barely spoke, glum and solemn. His depressed mood told me how much I meant to him. At the kitchen counter he buttered some toast, his mind somewhere else. I hugged him from behind, squeezing him tightly. "I'll see you soon," I said against his neck. "I'll call you every day. I promise."

"Promises," he mumbled. Turning slightly, he shoved a piece of toast in my mouth. "You better."

"I won't let you down."

I was supposed to leave at noon, but I ended up in bed with him again. Every time I said I was going, I stayed. I couldn't bring myself to say goodbye. Instead, as the sun set and Terry walked me to my car, I said, "Goodnight." To me, goodnight didn't have the same connotation as goodbye. To me, it implied I'd see him in the morning, and I was okay with that.

CHAPTER 21

22

Chapter 22

Scott

As I drove home, Terry's scent lingered. I could feel his breath against my neck. I wished I had stayed, but I owed it to Aimee to break up with her in person. And I needed to confront my parents. First Aimee, then my parents. I hated confrontation, and I feared this was going to get ugly.

After nearly a four hour drive home, I crawled into bed at one in the morning. Despite my exhaustion, I reached for my phone and called Terry. I just wanted to hear his voice before going to sleep.

"Hello?" he answered in a raspy voice as if he had just woken up from a deep sleep.

"Hey. It's Scott. I... I... I just wanted to say goodnight and I'll see you soon."

"Okay," he yawned. "Goodnight." He hung up before I did.

Just like any other Monday, I went to work, but I couldn't focus, thinking about Terry and Aimee. Unlike my usual self, I worked at a much slower pace. It was hard to stay motivated considering I didn't plan on working there much longer. Tonight I planned on breaking up with Aimee. I couldn't put it off anymore.

My dad always noticed everything, especially my lack of enthusiasm for work. "What's with you?" he asked as I stared out the window at my desk, biting the tip of my pen. "I thought you'd be relaxed and refreshed after a week off."

I only took five days off, but I wasn't in the mood to argue with him. "I'm trying to concentrate," I stated, a blatant lie.

"You're not trying hard enough," he said. "This is what happens when people take vacations. It takes days to catch up."

Eager to see me, Aimee showed up at the office at five o'clock. She was so excited, she didn't notice I didn't kiss her back. She hoped to go to her apartment after dinner to "make up for lost time," she said. My heart, body, and soul belonged to Terry, so I took her out to dinner instead.

The truth was about to come out on its own without me saying anything. Aimee knew me well enough to know something was on my mind. Usually famished after work, tonight I only picked at my salad.

"Okay, Scott, what's wrong?" she asked.

At first I said nothing, avoiding her eyes as I took a sip of wine.

"You've barely said anything all night," she said. "Tell me what's wrong."

My eyes wandered around the restaurant as I downed my whole glass of wine.

"You're kind of scaring me, Scott," she said as I poured another glass. "What's going on?"

"Aimee," I started. "I... I have to tell you something."

"Uh-oh. Why do I have a feeling this is a bad something?"

As I was about to come out to my girlfriend, the corners of her eyes filled with water as if she sensed what was coming.

"What's her name?" she asked, assuming I was about to tell her I was having an affair. She had no reason to believe my affair was with a man.

"Terry," I answered.

"Terry?" she scoffed. "Is she another intern? I know what your dad's interns are like."

"He's not an intern."

"What do you mean *he*? Terry's a man?"

"I wasn't expecting to see him again, but then we ran into each other, and we spent a few days together in—"

Aimee cut me off in mid-sentence. "Are you telling me I've been dating a gay man for the past two years?"

"Yes," I admitted. "I'm sorry. I'm not proud of myself."

"Shut up, Scott. You should have been honest with me in the first place."

"It's not like I don't care about you," I continued, trying to make myself feel better for breaking a decent woman's heart. "You're a really good person, and I'm sure you'll make someone happy someday."

"Do you love him?"

"Yes. Very much."

"I can't believe this is happening to me," she said, looking down at the table.

"Do you want me to take you home?" I asked, not sure what else to say or do.

"No. I'll take a taxi. Stay away from me."

As a parting gift, Aimee dumped her glass of wine in my lap. I deserved it. With my lap dripping in red wine, I continued to sit at the table, long after Aimee left. By myself, I finished the bottle of wine, tempted to order another but decided against it. I had to go home and talk to my parents before Aimee told her mother, who would then tell my mother. Slightly inebriated, I almost hit my mother's car in the driveway. As I staggered into the house, I told myself I'd never drive drunk again. I told myself a lot of things, though.

Reeking of red wine, I walked into the living room where my mother sat on one end of the couch, babbling to a friend on the phone while my dad sat on the other end, reading a newspaper and listening to the news on TV.

"You're home early," he said, not looking up from the paper as I plopped down in the recliner.

I merely grunted in response.

"Did you drive home drunk?" my dad asked.

Again, another grunt.

"I can smell you from here," he said. "You haven't been right since you came back from your trip. Where'd you go, anyway?"

"Vermont," I answered.

My dad hesitated before responding "Oh, yeah? What were you doing in Vermont?"

"Visiting Terry Lachance. What'd you say to Frankie and Susan that would stop them from giving him my letters? Tell me."

"What are you talking about?" my mother said, hanging up the phone. I sensed she knew exactly what I was talking about.

"You went to Vermont to see that fairy?" my dad said.

"His name is Terry and he's a man, not a fairy," I said. "His parents wouldn't keep my letters from him unless there was a reason, so what the fuck did you do to them?"

"Watch your language," my mother had the nerve to say.

"Tell me," I demanded.

Again, my dad hesitated. "When we were kids, Frankie and I used to hang around an old, empty church. Hobos used to camp out there, but that didn't stop us from hanging out there, too. Frankie had this thing with fire and campfires. We'd sit outside in the back of the church and cook hot dogs over a fire, a fire that Frankie started. On a windy night, a spark hit the building. The wood was so old and rotting, the place lit up in seconds. The fire killed three men. Frankie's the one who lit the fire with his father's matches. I warned him, but he never listened to me. I'm the only one who knew what happened. Frankie wanted it to stay that way. If he was ever caught, he would have been charged with arson and murder."

"So you threatened to turn him in if we continued our relationship?" I said. My dad didn't respond, not like I expected a logical response. "Your blackmail didn't work, did it? Terry and I found each other again, anyway. There's nothing you can do now. Frankie's dead. So what'd you do with my mail? I know you did something with it."

"We had it all diverted to home," my mother confessed.

"I should have known," I said, shaking my head. "Instead, I lost ten years. I'm not going to miss another ten."

"We did it for your own good," my mother said.

I had never hated my parents as much as I hated them right then. After an awkward pause, my mother spoke again.

"He wrote you hundreds of letters. Come with me."

"Nancy," my dad warned her as she headed out of the living room. I followed her up the stairs and to my parents' bedroom where she removed two large shoeboxes from the top of her closet.

"He must have written to you every day," she said, handing me the shoeboxes. "I don't understand how you could love a man when you have a beautiful woman like Aimee. You could have such a wonderful life together with children, a family of your own, a successful career. Why would you choose to live a life as an outcast? You could get AIDS or some other disease, not to mention you'd have no family or children."

"That's what you think," I said. "Maybe Terry is enough for me. I don't have HIV or AIDS and neither does Terry. I'm sick and tired of people assuming all gay men will get AIDS. Yeah, I'm gay, okay? Accept it or don't. I love Terry and he loves me. We belong together, and Aimee and I don't."

"What the hell are you going to do with Terry Lachance?" my dad scoffed in the doorway of their bedroom.

"Maybe live happily ever after," I said. "I can only hope. I'm going to Terry."

"If you go to him, don't ever come back," my dad said. "Consider yourself fired."

I expected this reaction, although I had hoped for something different. "Well, I'll be in Vermont, so I'd have to quit, anyway."

"I wish you'd think about this," my mother said.

"I spent the last ten years thinking about it."

"You're too drunk to drive," my dad said. "Pack up and get your ass out of here first thing in the morning."

On my way to my room, I stopped in the hallway with the shoeboxes in my arms. "Terry's a really good person," I said. "He's probably too good for me, but he wants me. Excuse me, I have some packing to do."

Instead of packing, I decided to read Terry's letters.

Dear Scott,

This is the last letter I'll ever write you as much as it hurts. It hurts even more that I haven't heard from you in two years. I hope you're happy with whatever life you've chosen. I don't think I could ever be happy without you. If I ever did anything to hurt you, I'm sorry. I wish you all the happiness and love in the world.

Terry

Terry was truly one of a kind, and there was no way I could let him go. By the time I reached the last letter, I had sobered up. To distract myself, I tossed my clothes into suitcases. I dug out some boxes from the basement and shoved everything I owned into them. Whatever didn't fit in my car I left on the curb for my parents to do whatever the hell they wanted with them. With a thermos filled with coffee, I was on the road around midnight. I wished I could have teleported myself to Vermont.

At three thirty in the morning, both the inn and Terry's house were pitch black, causing me to trip several times. He didn't respond to either the doorbell or my knocking. Desperate to see him, I resorted to pounding on the door.

Thirty minutes later, the door opened, and Terry stood behind the screen door, disheveled and bleary-eyed, in only a pair of boxers. "Hi," I said.

Confused, scratching the back of his head, he took a step backwards, allowing me to enter. We stared at each other silently for a few seconds. As Terry folded his arms over his bare chest, I couldn't tell what he was thinking. "You're late," he said.

"Yeah, I'm sorry. I... uh... I..."

"Fuck it." He threw his arms around me. "I don't care. You're here. Are you here to stay?"

"Yes."

We devoured each other in kisses, as if we hadn't seen each other in years instead of two days. My hands worked quickly, tugging down his boxers. As he stepped out of them, he tore open my shirt, pushing me against the kitchen counter. His hands shook as he undid my red wine stained pants. "I always wanted to get naked in my kitchen," Terry said. "I'm so glad you're here. So glad... "

"Yeah, me too."

"I knew you'd make the right decision," he said in between kisses. "Let's go upstairs."

Waking up to Terry, knowing I'd be waking up to him every day, seemed too unreal, like I was living in a fantasy world. I wanted to prove to him and everyone else that I was strong enough for this type of relationship. I knew, beyond a reasonable doubt, that I made the right decision, that I made the best decision of my life.

For the first time in a very long time, I slept soundly, and it wasn't just because Terry and I didn't get to sleep until six in the morning. When I opened my eyes, I found Terry leaning on his elbow, staring down at me. I didn't move, my brown eyes fixed with his blue ones.

"Hey," I said. "Am I going to wake up to you staring at me every morning?" I teased him. "I love waking up to you, but it's creepy, you staring at me like that. Was I snoring?"

"No," he said, caressing the side of my head. "I want to spend the rest of my life with you. I'd propose to you if we could get married."

"And I'd say yes."

He kissed me and rested his head on my chest. "This is going to work. Us. It's going to work."

Smiling, I kissed the top of his head, knowing he was right, convinced this relationship could withstand anything.

23

Chapter 23

1996
Scott

Waking up from a peaceful slumber, the blankets ruffled, a pair of wet lips toying with me down below. "Who's doing that?" I joked, stretching with a yawn. Slipping my hands under the blankets, I ran my fingers through Terry's hair. "What did I do to deserve this?" My legs trembled as Terry's lips closed around my cock. "You always give the best blow jobs," I said, throwing the covers on the floor. I liked to watch him. He'd suck and suck until I came, then finish inside me. This morning was no different, but this bed was different. I was back in my hometown, five miles from my childhood home, spending the weekend in a hotel. If Mike hadn't asked me to be his best man, I doubted I'd be here right now.

Even if he hadn't asked me to be his best man, I probably still would have come because Terry would never let me blow off my only brother's wedding. In a few hours I'd have to face my parents after six years of silence.

Terry released my cock and snaked up my body, planting a kiss on my lips. "Do you want me to fuck you now or do you just want to take a shower and get some breakfast?" Terry asked, his lips against the side of my neck.

"How about both?"

"We can do that."

"I love the way you fuck," I laughed as he thrust inside me. I slid my hands down his back, culminating at his ass. I loved these mornings.

But then reality set in, and I had to face the fact I hadn't written that traditional best man's speech. I was always such a gifted procrastinator. As Terry brushed his teeth, I sat in the crappy hotel chair, staring at a blank piece of paper.

"Hey, Terry, could you do me a favor?" With a toothbrush in his mouth, he peeked out of the bathroom. "Could you write my speech? You're much better with words than I am."

"I'm not writing your speech," he mumbled with a mouth full of toothpaste. "You had months to work on this speech."

I scribbled down some ideas and concluded I'd have to wing most of it, hoping I wouldn't stutter and make a fool out of myself. I never had a stuttering problem unless I was in front of a group of people. My nerves sometimes got the better of me. I even procrastinated getting dressed. Terry had to hurry me along, which was nothing new. I'd be lost without him.

"You need to relax," Terry said on the way to the church. I sat in the passenger's side of the car, clutching the door handle, staring out the window. The stupid speech wasn't the only thing on my mind.

"I don't want my family to treat you like shit," I said.

"Mike doesn't treat me like shit."

Every summer for the past two years, Mike and his fiancée, Michelle, spent a week in Vermont. Last year Mike blew off our parents and shared Thanksgiving with us, which didn't bode well with them, or so I was told. If they would just accept Terry and our relationship, I'd let everything else go.

"I'm not expecting a warm handshake from your dad or a hug from your mother," he said.

"My mother doesn't hug," I reminded him.

"You know what I mean. You look great in that tux, by the way."

"Yeah, so do you."

"I'm not wearing a tux."

"Well, you look great in that suit. Thanks for coming."

"I consider myself part of your family and so does Mike. You know what I'm going to do today? I'm going to get you good and drunk. We're gonna have a lot of fun."

Knowing Terry, he'd follow through with his plan and I looked forward to it.

In the church, Tommy and Nancy sat in the front pew, a picture perfect couple. They hadn't aged much over the years. Before the ceremony started, Terry approached my parents, extending his hand to shake my dad's, but he didn't even acknowledge him. Without batting an eye, Terry walked away, choosing to sit in the bride's section. Mike immediately went to my parents. Judging by his exaggerated hand gestures and facial expressions, he was giving them a scolding as if they were two naughty children.

Our parents merely nodded at me. I didn't expect much more than that. Both beamed with pride as the stunning bride made her way down the aisle with her father. They'd never beam with such pride for me. I'd given up on making them happy, focusing on my happiness instead of theirs.

The reception was held at my parents' country club. I hadn't set foot in the club since Mike's graduation party.

Getting ready for the best man's speech, I graciously accepted a glass of champagne, looking down at the scribbles on my scrap of paper. I glanced at Terry, then Mike, and crumpled it up. I decided to speak from the heart. I had a lot of fond memories of our adventures and shenanigans. Most importantly, Mike was supportive of me and Terry and accepted us. For years, he'd been trying to facilitate the mending of my relationship with my parents, but they wouldn't budge an inch.

Leave it to Mike to seat Terry and I at the same table with our parents and other extended family members. I hadn't seen my eighty-year-old Aunt Corinne in twenty years. And then there was my aunt Cathy, my dad's older sister, who was even snobbier than my mother. I could only imagine what she thought of Terry.

To everyone at the table, my mother introduced Terry as my "friend" and "roommate." As she bragged about my success as a graphic designer in Vermont— which she learned from Mike—I squirmed in my seat, accepting another glass of champagne from the waitress.

"Chill," Terry whispered in my ear, squeezing my knee.

I couldn't "chill" because Terry wasn't my friend or roommate, and I didn't want anyone to think that.

"Mom, Terry's not my roommate," I said, raising my voice so everyone could hear me over the chatter and music. "He's my partner, and I don't mean business partner. We share a house together, my name's on the deed, and we sleep in the same bed."

"Can't we just enjoy this day without controversy?" my mother said. "Show a little respect. This isn't about you."

"Come on, let's dance," Terry said, grabbing my hand and pulling me to my feet. "I'd appreciate it if you'd lead since I suck at it. You need to relax."

"How can you be so calm?" I asked as Terry placed his hand in the center of my back on the dance floor. "Doesn't it bother you that my dad refused to shake your hand, that my mother referred to you as my friend and roommate?"

"Yeah, it bothers me, but I'm not going to let a bunch of ignorant people ruin my day. I'm having a good time."

"I don't want people to think you're my roommate."

"No one thinks that. Look at us, Scott. We're the only two guys dancing together. We're clearly not roommates. I love this song."

He referred to Louis Armstrong's *Wonderful World.* I loved the song, too. It relaxed me.

"You know I'd marry you if I could," Terry said.

"I know," I said. "Would you get down on one knee?"

"Yes."

"I bet you would," I said and kissed his cheek.

Later, as I danced with the bride, I spotted Terry talking with my dad for the first time that day. Neither looked particularly unhappy or angry. I wondered if Terry re-approached him because he never gave up easily, determined to win my dad over. I figured I'd hear all about their conversation tonight in bed. Many serious conversations took place in bed at night.

After a day of drinking and dancing, the romance continued in our hotel room. "Scott, what did my dad do?" Terry asked amid drunken love making.

"What do you mean?" I responded, enjoying his dick deep inside me, my long legs wrapped around his body.

"Your dad said something to me today when you were dancing with Michelle."

"Can we talk about that later?"

I had never told Terry about his father's dark secret. I didn't see the point. Instead, I just told him my dad threatened to shut down the Inn and Cottages. Terry never asked any more questions, just happy that we were together.

Terry sucked my bottom lip, his body trembling as he came hard inside me. "Okay, tell me now."

"I love you," I said, hugging him. "I wouldn't mind getting down on one knee."

"You're avoiding the question."

"It doesn't matter what he did. My dad was egging you on just to upset you. He doesn't know what an incredible person you are."

"Stop protecting my dad," he said, withdrawing. "I deserve to know, Scott, and I wished you hadn't lied to me."

"Because it didn't matter."

"It matters now. I don't want any secrets between us."

I couldn't argue with him because he was right. I didn't want any secrets, either. Because I was still hard and happily inebriated, I wasn't in the mood to tell the story at the moment, but I didn't have a choice if I wanted to come at some point tonight.

"Please tell me, Scott."

"Fine," I sighed. "Your dad was a kid when it happened. He accidentally lit fire to an old, vacant church, only it wasn't vacant, and he killed three people. They were homeless and had been living there, but our dads didn't know it. The men burned in the fire. My dad is the only one who knows about it. Your dad didn't want you to know."

"My dad lived with that on his conscience his entire life?"

"I guess so. I don't know any other details, except that he was afraid my dad would tell you and other people that could potentially destroy his business, or something like that. See, it doesn't change anything. Do you feel better now that you know? No, it doesn't look like you do."

"Do you think my mom knew?"

"No, I don't."

"I wish you hadn't told me," he said, sitting cross-legged. "Because it doesn't change anything. It was an accident, right?"

"Yes. Even my dad says it was an accident."

"But your dad threatened my dad. Maybe he was going to claim it wasn't an accident."

"To be honest, Terry, my dad's an asshole, but I don't think he would have actually said your dad burned the church on purpose. I think his bark is bigger than his bite, but your dad didn't want to take any chances. He could have been charged with arson and murder. Don't be mad at me."

"I'm not mad at you. You were protecting me and my father's memory. I get it." I squeezed the back of his neck as he looked down and away.

"Your dad was still a great guy," I said. "I wish I got to know him better."

"Yeah," he said. "Me, too. No more secrets?"

"No more secrets," I said and kissed him. I uncrossed his legs and got on top of him. "Just remember your dad as a good man."

He nodded, kissing my mouth. I clasped my hands in his and brought his arms over his head.

"You know you're my better half, right?" I said. "I love you, and I'm glad you're here with me, but I can't wait to go home." I didn't even make it inside him when I lost it.

"It's okay," Terry said. "There's always tomorrow."

"Yeah, tomorrow," I sighed, resting my head on his shoulder. I couldn't imagine my life with anyone else but Terry.

24

Chapter 24

2003
Scott

Trees glistened with newly fallen snow as I drove up the country roads on my way home after a long day at work. I never liked snow, but I couldn't deny its beauty.

On the front stoop, I stomped the snow off my boots, noticing that something was different about our new screen door. Scratching my head, I opened the inside door, only to step outside again. Someone had cut a hole in the center, and I suspected the culprit was inside.

"Hey, Terry, do you know—" In mid-sentence, I stopped in the living room, finding Terry and twelve-year-old Ariel dropping towels on our two thousand dollar Persian rug. In the middle of the coffee table sat a three foot tall clay volcano that Ariel made for his science fair project. Red liquid dripped out of it, trickling onto the carpet. Both Terry and Ariel attempted to clean it up before I got home. I had a hunch that Ariel also used part of the screen for his experiment. Terry and I told him to work on his project outside or in the kitchen and not in the living room.

In front of the coffee table, headless barbie dolls scattered the couch, their heads on the floor splattered with that red liquid. Our six-week-old infant, Paul, lay in his bassinet, stirring, sensing my presence.

"Sorry," Terry said. "Things got a little out of hand." Although he operated a summer camp for kids, he had little control over our own kids, and things tended to "get out of hand" very quickly. I never knew what I'd find when I got home, especially when Terry was in charge.

Two years ago, Terry and I became foster parents to Ariel, a former camper, and his half sister, Luna. After we solidified our civil union in 2002, we adopted them. While it wasn't always easy, we had more good times than bad times.

Until we had kids, I always thought Terry was perfect — he was handsome, smart, funny and witty, a talented singer and guitarist, and caring and compassionate. He was always carefree and laid back, things I loved about him. But Ariel and Luna didn't respond to his lackadaisical type of parenting. Without structure and boundaries, they'd run the house—and us—into the ground.

And besides his laissez-faire style of parenting, he couldn't change a diaper to save his life.

"Where's Luna?" I asked.

"Crying like a little baby," Ariel said, his dark hair and clothes coated in tomato juice. "She ate all my candy."

"So you decapitated her dolls' heads?" I asked.

"Yeah, they had a big fight," Terry said.

Before I lost my temper at the disaster on the floor and the destruction of our brand new screen door, I headed upstairs to find Luna.

I had to cut Terry some slack, though, because he was also dealing with Paul while supervising an oftentimes unruly Ariel. Terry was the most likeable, most gentle man I'd ever known, yet Paul had an adverse reaction to him, making him question his parental capabilities. He cried every time Terry picked him up.

Down the hall, I followed the little girl's cries, locating seven-year-old Luna under her bed, hugging a teddy bear.

"Hi, there," I said, kneeling on the floor, peeking under the bed.

"Hi, Papi," she cried. Even though Terry spoke fluent Spanish, Luna called me "Papi" from the minute we adopted her while Terry was "Dad" or "Daddy."

"What's going on?" I asked.

"Ariel killed my dolls," she said.

"He didn't kill your dolls. I can fix them. Come out and help me make dinner."

As Paul's cries grew louder, I knew Terry was on his way to Luna's bedroom. "Are you mad?" he asked, standing in the doorway with Paul.

"We told Ariel to work on his project outside or in the kitchen. Did you know he cut a hole in our brand new screen door?"

"Screens are inexpensive to replace, and you don't know if the rug is destroyed. We might be able to clean it."

"That's not the point. Ariel didn't listen to us. He did what he wanted. What are you doing to Paul?" I said as the infant cried. "Give me the baby."

"I'm completely inept, aren't I?" he said, placing the baby in my arms.

"No, you're not completely inept. Well, maybe a little," I teased him, rocking Paul.

"How do you do that?" My ability to soothe Paul both fascinated and infuriated Terry. I never thought I'd be much of a father, afraid I'd take after my own, but it turned out not to be the case.

"He's hungry," I said as Paul sucked my finger.

"I fed him an hour ago."

"Well, he's still hungry." Amid the Lachance-Prescott madness, the doorbell rang. Every day was an adventure. "Are you expecting someone?"

"No. I'll get it. Go feed Paul. He hates me, anyway."

"He doesn't hate you," I told him not-so-convincingly.

While I prepared the bottle in the kitchen, Luna shadowed me, following me around the house until I fixed her dolls. Holding Paul, I wandered into the living room to get a better look at the damage.

"Damn," I said, examining the destruction. "We should think about getting a plastic coffee table, or maybe we can cover our furniture with plastic. My grandmother used to do that. What about yours?"

"Um... uh... Scott, you have company," Terry said.

Dressed in a Burberry coat and matching scarf, a Coach bag hanging from her shoulder, not a piece of her dyed auburn hair out of place, my mother stood by the front door, the first time I'd seen her in person in seven years. Every now and again, I'd call her, or she'd call me. I hadn't spoken to my father since Mike's wedding.

"Mom," I said, not sure what to say. The house was in utter disarray and in no condition for company. Growing up, my mother forbade toys in the living room. The house was like a museum, everything pristine and in perfect order. My house looked nothing like my childhood home.

"I'm leaving your father," she stated, not noticing my embarrassingly messy living room, nor did she notice the baby in my arms.

"Oh, okay," I said, looking to Terry for help. He was good at rescuing me in awkward situations. Terry, too, was at a loss for words, staring at my mother with little expression on his face. The last time he saw her, she snubbed him. "It would have been nice if you called first. We don't exactly live around the corner from you." In fact, I lived four hours from my hometown of Newton, Massachusetts.

"I needed to get away," she said.

"So you came to Vermont in the middle of February?" My mother was never an outdoorsy type of person unless it involved sunbathing with a white wine spritzer and a good romance novel in her hands. "You don't even ski."

"Daddy, can we go skiing tomorrow?" Luna asked. She loved all sports, particularly ice skating and skiing. Terry was an excellent skier while I was an avid runner and swimmer. I hated the snow.

"Sure," Terry said. "Please, have a seat," he said to my mother. "I'll take your coat." She took off her coat and handed it to Terry. With Paul in one arm, I pushed the dolls aside on the couch, making room for her.

"This is Paul," I said, "and that's Luna and Ariel. Ariel, Luna, this is my mother."

I'd told her about our adopted children, but she never commented. I didn't know if she accepted them and considered them her grandchildren. Was she Grandma or Nana, or was she Nancy or Mrs. Prescott?

"Grammy!" Luna exclaimed, making the decision for all of us. Nancy Prescott was neither a Grandma nor a Nana but a Grammy. "I'm Luna."

"Hello, Luna," she said, clutching the strap of her bag, perhaps second guessing her decision to visit me without notice.

"And you thought I'd never have a family," I said.

"When did you get a baby?"

"I told you Terry and I were adopting Ariel and Luna's brother." At the start of Rosa Gomez's second trimester, she called us from prison to ask if we'd adopt her baby, her eighth child. For the past five years, she'd been in and out of prison and was now serving a twenty-year sentence for a variety of offences.

"He's a beautiful baby," my mother said.

"And Scott's a natural," Terry said. "I mean, he's a great father." My cheeks burned, never comfortable accepting compliments. "Excuse the mess. Ariel's science fair project worked really well."

"Terry, maybe you should start dinner," I said, even though it was my turn to make dinner. Without Terry's intermittent interjecting, I wanted to talk to my mother alone, to find out what really possessed her to come to my house instead of Mike's, and why she decided to "leave" my father at sixty-six years old.

"Come on, guys," Terry said to Ariel and Luna.

"I don't want to help," Ariel said.

"Go help," I instructed him. "You're already on thin ice for the tomato juice lava and barbie doll decapitation."

"It was tomato sauce," Ariel said. "Dad gave it to me. He said it was okay."

"Yeah, well, Dad's grounded, too."

Ariel sighed, rolling his eyes, as he followed Terry and Luna to the kitchen. My mother's eyes gravitated from Luna to Paul. "Would you like to hold him?" I asked her.

"If you wouldn't mind," she said. I transferred him into her arms. "So you and him... he... " She hesitated as if Terry was a dirty word.

"His name is Terry and you know it. Remember, this is our home, so I'd appreciate it if you show some respect."

"And it's an interesting home, too." Her eyes wandered around the room, drawn to the family photos on the wall. "So you and Terry really adopted these children together?"

"Yes," I said. "Why are you leaving Dad? Did he do something?" I wondered if he was having an affair.

"I want your father to retire."

"You're leaving him after forty-five years of marriage because he won't retire? Dad won't ever retire."

"I know," she sighed. "And I also wanted to see you. It's been such a long time. This feud has been going on long enough."

"It's not a feud. I've invited you and Dad here lots of times. Terry's not going anywhere, and neither am I."

"I tell your father that all the time."

"So why didn't you come sooner?"

"Would you mind if I stayed in the inn tonight?" she asked, avoiding my question. "It's such a long ride back."

"I thought you left Dad. Why would you go back?"

"I told him to pack his bags and get out, so he better not be there when I return."

"Why didn't you go to Mike's? He only lives twenty minutes away from you."

"I didn't want to go to Mike's."

"Why?"

"Because I wanted to see my other son. I gave birth to two boys, you know."

Since Terry was so insistent on being a good host—or maybe he was just being nosy—he re-entered the living room with a bottle of wine. "I thought you might like a drink," Terry said. He was thinking of me more than my mother. He had an uncanny ability to read my mind.

"Thanks," I said, accepting the glass from Terry.

"Can I ask you something, Scott?" my mother asked as Terry left the room. "When did you realize you were a homosexual?"

I heard Terry giggle from the kitchen. My mother had never asked me this question before.

"I had feelings for men way before I met Terry, if that's what you're asking."

"But you dated such pretty girls."

"And Terry's a pretty man." I laughed at my joke. I always told Terry he had "pretty blue eyes."

"He is handsome," my mother said. The compliment caught me by surprise, considering she rarely paid anyone a compliment.

"Yes, he is."

After finishing his bottle, Paul dozed off in my mother's arms. "Are you happy?" she asked me.

"Yes, I'm very happy. Terry's a good man. He's not a deadbeat beatnik. He works hard, much harder than I ever worked. Do you love Dad?"

"We've been married for forty-five years."

"But do you love him?"

"Of course I love him. I wanted to meet my other grandchildren. I always wanted a granddaughter. It doesn't look like Mike plans on having any more children." Mike had two sons, five-year-old Tyler and two-year-old Charlie. "Maybe I could take Luna shopping some time?"

"She'd love that," I said. "She loves shopping."

I doubted my mother planned on divorcing my father, but I believed she wanted to see me and meet my children.

In an attempt to impress my mother, Terry made his infamous veggie lasagna. Throughout dinner, Luna did most of the talking, monopolizing the conversation. She volunteered information while my mother had to pry information out of Ariel. Monosyllabic, he answered my mother's questions.

"What grade are you in?" she asked.

"Sixth," he answered.

"What's your favorite subject?"

"Science."

"Do you play any sports?"

"No."

"Where are you from?" So far tonight, she stayed away from asking overly personal questions until now.

"Huh?" he responded.

"You're not from Vermont, are you?"

"They were born in Boston," I said, hoping she wouldn't ask questions about their biological mother. In and out of foster homes since he was six, Ariel resented her and didn't trust any adult until he attended summer camp two years ago. Terry and I worked hard to gain Ariel's trust. The phone saved us from further pre-adoption questions. Terry got up to answer it, returning seconds later, color drained from his face.

"Your husband would like to talk to you," Terry said to my mother.

"I have nothing to say to him," she said, bringing her glass of wine to her lips. To save Terry from talking to my dad again, I went to the kitchen and told him exactly what my mother said.

"Put her on the damn phone," my father said.

"It's nice to talk to you, too," I said facetiously. "We're in the middle of dinner, so could you call back later?"

"No, put her on the phone, Scottie. I'm not hanging up until I talk to her."

In frustration, I dropped the receiver, letting it hang from the kitchen wall. "I can't believe I'm in the middle of their bullshit quarrel," I whispered to Terry, sitting back down at the table. "Go talk to him," I said to my mother. "He said he won't stop calling until you talk to him."

"Very well," she said, tossing her napkin on her plate.

"This is so weird," I said to Terry, who snickered under his breath. Five minutes later, my mother sat back down at the table.

"It looks like I'm going back to your father tomorrow," she said. "He's thinking about coming to see you—if you'll have him—and he's also taking me to Las Vegas. I always wanted to go there."

"That sounds good," I said with a forced smile. Not much had changed; she was easily bought.

After Luna talked my mother's ear off, Terry brought her to one of the many vacant rooms in the inn. She was polite to him and said "thank you." I couldn't have asked for anything more than that.

"That was one of the weirdest experiences of my life," Terry said in our bedroom. "It almost made you forget about the volcano incident."

"Why'd you have to remind me?" I said, falling into bed. "I haven't seen my mother in seven years, and she shows up out of the blue because she's leaving my dad, and then she agrees to go back because he's taking her to Vegas? How am I even related to her? To them?"

"I've asked myself that a million times. Is tonight a pajama optional night?"

"If you want. Let's hope Paul sleeps for more than two hours."

"We don't need two hours." Stark naked, Terry approached the bed. He yanked my pajama bottoms off as I threw my t-shirt on the floor.

Seconds after Terry's lips landed on my cock, Paul wailed down the hall. If Terry hadn't locked the door, Ariel would have burst into our room, angry that Paul woke him up again. Terry released my cock and thrust inside me, determined to get some action, which didn't happen too often lately. We finished just in time before Ariel pounded on our door. Terry had it easy; he'd roll over and go to sleep while I soothed and/or fed Paul. Parenthood had its good and bad moments, and I wouldn't have changed anything.

25

Chapter 25

2009

Terry

Something was happening today, and I couldn't remember what it was. Here I was, lying in bed on this important day, yet I couldn't say what was so important about it. The aroma of blueberry pancakes and coffee aroused me from a deep sleep, although I couldn't open my eyes or drag myself out of bed on this cold, dreary Sunday morning.

"Hey," Scott whispered in my ear, his fingertips brushing over my waist, tickling me ever so slightly. "Guess what today is?"

"I didn't miss your birthday again, did I?" I said with my eyes closed. For the first time ever, I forgot Scott's birthday, and I'd never live it down.

"No. My birthday's in June. Today is November twenty-second."

November twenty-second sounded familiar. *What happened on November twenty-second?*

"November twenty-second," I thought for a minute, rolling over to face him. A tray sat on the bedside table with a mound of pancakes, a cup of coffee, and two mimosas. In the center of the pancakes were two unlit candles: a five and a zero. "Shit. It's my birthday."

Scott said fifty was just a number, but it was easy for him to say considering he was forty-eight. There was a reason I forgot this birthday.

"Please don't sing to me," I said. As much as I loved Scott, I didn't love his singing.

"Happy birthday," he said and kissed me. "You don't look a day over thirty."

"You're such a liar."

"Would I lie to you?"

"Yes, to make me feel better."

"Well, I'm not lying. Here," he said, handing me a mimosa. As I brought the champagne flute to my lips, Scott pulled out a small gift bag from the drawer of the nightstand. "Happy birthday. Wait... don't open it yet."

"Oh, no," I smiled as Scott got down on one knee. "I can't believe you beat me to it." A few months ago, Vermont legalized gay marriage. Despite our civil union, we always said we'd get married if we could. I never thought Scott would propose to me first. I forgot all about it.

"You got me a ring, too?" I said, peeking in the bag.

"You can't propose without a ring. Will you marry me, Terry?"

"Come here," I said.

"Answer me, Terry."

"Come here," I repeated, pulling him to me. He lay on top of me, propped on his elbows. I cupped his chin in my palms. "Yes, of course I'll marry you. I love you, and I love the ring."

"You're still so fucking sexy," he said, bringing his lips to mine. "My mom's here. She's taking Paul and Luna out so I can pleasure you all day."

"I never thought your mother would come in handy."

"She's mellowed in her old age."

For the past six years, Nancy Prescott took an active part in our lives. She had softened and almost accepted me as Scott's significant other, his soon-to-be husband. Tom Prescott still hadn't come around.

"Will you pleasure me now? I need it."

"I love your body," he said.

I enjoyed an early morning blow job and everything that came after. I could imagine no other lover but Scott. The pancakes were cold by the time we got to them but having Scott for breakfast was just as good.

* * *

After finishing the grocery shopping for Thanksgiving, Paul and I walked into the house to find Luna sobbing on the couch. Overly dramatic and extra sensitive, she had an emotional breakdown at least once a week. I wondered what today's travesty was. "What happened?" I asked.

"Papi's a jerk," she cried.

"Why is he a jerk now?"

Ironically, Luna and Scott were very close. Both avid runners, they ran at least ten races together. Scott was also overprotective and sometimes too strict, but he usually had a reason to ground her.

"He grounded me for a month."

"Did he tell you why?"

"Colby and I were hanging out in my room. We weren't doing anything. I swear." Both beautiful and outgoing, Luna had a new boyfriend every week. They were innocent little crushes, but Scott was having a hard time with it. He didn't want our kids to grow up.

"You were just hanging out?"

"Yes," she sniffed.

I suspected she and Colby were doing something else other than just "hanging out."

"Let me talk to Papi. Help Paul put the food away," I said. I didn't trust a six-year-old to put the food away by himself. "And get Ariel. He can help, too."

As Luna headed to the kitchen, I searched the house for Scott. Having just returned from a run, I found him in the bathroom, stepping out of the shower.

"Hey," he said. "How was the store? I bet it was crazy, huh?"

I wasn't there in the steamy hot bathroom to talk about the insanity of the people in the grocery store two days before Thanksgiving. "You can't ground Luna for a month," I said as he wrapped a towel around his waist.

"She was kissing a boy in her room. What have we said about boys in her room?"

"We said it was okay as long as the door was open. Was the door closed?"

"No."

"Then you have no reason to ground her. You're totally overreacting."

"It's not just that," he said. "She's getting out of control. Don't you remember she was out until eleven last month on a school night? She never texted or called. Nothing. She's thirteen, Terry! That's not okay."

Wow, he's fiery tonight, I thought while also wondering what he was talking about. He never told me she was out until eleven. "When was she out until eleven?" I asked.

"Last month. You were about to call the police. How could you forget?"

"Oh, yeah," I lied. I had no recollection of that night. No wonder Scott was so angry. I could never let him know I forgot because he'd never let me live it down. "But a month is still a little harsh. We don't want her to rebel even more."

"Yeah, fine. I just don't want her getting into trouble."

"I know," I said, squeezing his shoulder.

"My dad's coming for Thanksgiving," he stated, walking out of the bathroom. Every year for the past six years, his father said he was coming for Thanksgiving but backed out at the last minute. For reasons I never understood, Scott desperately wanted him to accept us. "I'll talk to Luna. She's so over the top about everything."

"Good luck with that," I said. As he entered our bedroom, he stuck his tongue out at me.

* * *

The day before Thanksgiving, I gathered up all the ingredients for my mother's pumpkin pie, something I'd been making since I was a kid. Suddenly I had a brain freeze and couldn't recall how much brown sugar and butter to use. What about eggs? How many eggs did I need?

"Hey, Scott, do you remember my mother's pumpkin pie recipe?" I asked as he sat at the kitchen table playing Uno with Paul.

"No. You always made the pie. You need to write things down."

"Yeah, I know, Getting old sucks."

"You're not old. You just have a lot on your mind."

I googled another recipe I hoped resembled my mother's. I wanted everything to go smoothly just in case Tom Prescott showed up.

"You need to relax," Scott said. Always perceptive, he knew when I was stressed. "Everything's cool. No one will know you couldn't remember your mother's recipe... everyone except Ariel. That kid notices everything."

If my mother's pumpkin pie recipe was the only thing I'd forgotten I wouldn't have been so upset. I forgot Scott's birthday last June. I'd never forgotten a birthday in my life, and I missed important financial deadlines, nearly putting the camp at risk. Every year, I reapplied for government grants that kept the camp running and allowed me to give scholarships to kids in need. Fortunately, I received consistent donations from a variety of businesses and individuals, so I didn't rely solely on government funds, but it made things tight. Overworked and stressed, I hired an assistant to help Angie, my business partner, and myself. I should have hired an assistant years ago.

While I made dessert, Scott cooked the turkey, which I didn't eat since I was still a vegetarian, but it smelled damn good. Scott lived for Thanksgiving. He'd get up at the butt crack of dawn just to prepare the turkey.

Luna ran down the stairs, the first to answer the door. "Dad! Papi! Grammy's here with some old guy."

"What's she talking about?" Scott asked, basting the turkey.

"Some old guy? Do you think she's talking about your dad?" I said.

"You think so?" Scott put the turkey back in the oven and went to the front door. His father had never set foot in our house. Here he was, nearly twenty years after the first time we met, standing at the front door. "Dad," he said, stunned and dumbfounded, yet strangely calm. "Happy Thanksgiving. Thanks for coming. I can see you met Luna."

"Is this Grandpa?" Luna asked. My mother hugged her, stepping into the living room.

"He's my father," Scott said.

"Can I come in?" Tom asked.

"Yeah, of course," Scott said. "Let me introduce you to everyone. You know Mike and Michelle," he joked. "That's Ariel, the oldest one, Luna and Paul, and you know Terry."

In the living room, Mike and his wife, Michelle, sat on the couch while their two boys played a game of Chutes and Ladders with Paul. Eighteen-year-old Ariel was working on his fifth bacon-wrapped scallop that Scott made. The holidays were the one time of year where Scott made at least three dishes involving some sort of meat.

As I went to shake Tom's hand, he walked past me, snubbing me in my own home. Although Scott seethed with anger, he said nothing, biting his tongue.

"Don't be an ass, Dad," Mike spoke up instead. "Or you can leave."

"We drove all this way," he said. "We're not leaving."

"Sit down," Scott said.

"Please, make yourself at home," I added.

Although Tom wasn't particularly pleasant to me, I didn't see any point in being hostile to him. What kind of message would that send to our kids? Anyway, he took a big step in coming to our house. He may not have cared about me, but his presence led me to believe he still cared about Scott and was somewhat interested in how his life turned out.

To ease his nerves, Scott downed a shot of Crown Royal, his father's preferred whiskey. Sitting side by side, I squeezed Scott's knee to relax him. Tom's eyes shifted from my hand on Scott's knee to the painting above the fireplace, a Monet-style painting Scott did a few years ago of the family. I always said he was talented.

"So how's business?" Mike asked me.

"I can't complain," I answered. "Scott painted that," I said to Tom as his eyes remained fixed on the painting. "Pretty good, huh?"

"Is that how you make your living?" Tom asked Scott.

"No. I paint in my spare time," Scott answered. "I'm a graphic designer, remember?"

"I didn't think you still did that."

"He does pretty well," I said. We planned on using Scott's income for Ariel's upcoming college tuition.

"Dad, if you're going to sit there and pretend Terry's invisible, then I'd rather you not be here," Scott said.

"Come on, Tom, let me show you the kitchen and I'll make you a drink," Nancy said, standing up. With an exaggerated sigh, Tom reluctantly followed Nancy to the kitchen.

"Is it me or does he have a bug up his ass?" Ariel said. Mike laughed so hard he spit out his drink.

"That's not nice," Scott said.

"Even though it's true," Mike said.

Five minutes later, Nancy and Tom returned with cocktails in their hands. "Nice place you have here," Tom said. "Frankie would be proud."

That was the closest I'd ever get to a compliment. Whatever Nancy said to him worked. The more whiskey Tom drank, the more jovial he became. By the end of the day, Tom had almost accepted me as Scott's life partner and soon-to-be husband. Of course, he had a little help from Crown Royal.

26

Chapter 26

2015

Terry

Today wasn't the first day I drew a total blank, walking down a once familiar street that suddenly seemed not so familiar. I relied on my phone's GPS, but lately I had a habit of forgetting my phone on the kitchen table. Without it, I was screwed.

I had been going to Millie's Ice Cream Parlor since I was a kid. If Paul had a good week at school, I'd get him a pint of his favorite ice cream, cotton candy. Even at twelve, he looked forward to this treat, and it always had to be cotton candy.

But today I couldn't find Millie's. Nothing looked familiar. I walked down street after street, trying to find it, doing my best not to look like a total nutcase. Just last week I got lost driving home from the grocery store because I left my phone at home again, and there were other times and other places.

As afternoon turned into evening, I gave up on the ice cream, desperate to get home. On a beautiful late winter afternoon, I had walked the five miles from home to downtown. In the dark, I was afraid I'd get lost walking home. Here I was, a grown man, completely and utterly afraid. Petrified.

"Hey, Terry," a man said, approaching me on the street. "Did you walk here again?" This man acted like he knew me, yet I didn't know him. "Are you okay? It's me, Jim." He took off his baseball cap, revealing a shiny bald head. Without the hat, he became familiar.

"Jim... yeah," I said. "Hi, Jim, how are you?" I realized this was Jim Donnelly, someone who had been working for me for years. What did he do again? I paused, wrecking my brain, trying to figure out what he did. And then I remembered, *He's the groundskeeper.*

"It's getting late," Jim said. "I can give you a lift home if you want."

"That would be great," I said. "I didn't expect it to get so cold." I'd never let anyone know I got lost in my hometown.

Relieved, I got in his black pickup. As Jim dropped me off in front of the house, Scott swung open the door with Paul right behind him. This wasn't the first time I had been late without calling. It was after seven o'clock and I had been gone since three. I would have called if I had my phone.

"Where the hell have you been?" Scott was more concerned than angry.

"Jim gave me a ride home," I said.

"That doesn't explain where you've been."

"I'm starving. I'll make dinner." I ignored Scott's comment, walking past him and Paul. He'd never believe me if I told him I got lost. It sounded ludicrous, especially since I'd been living in this town my entire life.

"Terry?" Scott expected an answer from me.

"Dad, did you get the ice cream?" Paul asked.

Too many questions. Too many people talking, overwhelming me. I could barely keep it together. "No, I'm sorry," I said. "I forgot. I'll get some tomorrow."

"What?" Paul exclaimed, as if forgetting to buy his ice cream was a criminal offense. "You promised me."

"I forgot, okay?" I snapped, not usually one to lose my cool. "I told you I'll go tomorrow. The world doesn't revolve around you, does it?"

Seeking an explanation, Scott followed me into the kitchen. He stood in the doorway, staring at me as I searched the refrigerator for something to make for dinner. "Do we have chickpeas?" I asked.

"Yes," Scott replied. "But you won't find them in there."

"Well, where the hell are they?" I forgot where I last put them. Scott walked over to a cabinet and took out a can of chickpeas. Annoyed with me, he slammed the can down in front of me.

We had our share of blow outs over the years, and we were on the verge of having another one. Historically, our arguments never lasted long. Usually, Scott would storm out of the house, go for a long walk and come back remorseful and apologetic. He insisted on having the last word and believed he was always right.

"Where were you?" he asked again. I didn't respond, proceeding to open the can of chickpeas. "Maybe if you wouldn't forget your phone."

I just wanted him to shut up, but he kept going on and on, lecturing me like a child.

"You were late last week, too, and a couple of other times with no phone calls or texts," he said. "Nothing, not a word. What's going on, Terry? Tell me. Are you seeing someone? Is that it?"

"I'm going to pretend I didn't hear that," I said. I understood why he was so suspicious, but the accusation didn't hurt any less. Any rational person would have questioned my secretive, bizarre behaviors. Never in a million years would I consider being with someone else.

"Then why won't you tell me where you were?" he persisted.

I didn't know what to say. I felt like I was losing my mind and didn't know what to do about it. Scott worried about everything; I didn't want him to worry about me, too.

"Terry, you never kept anything from me before."

"Do we have any green chilies?"

"Yeah, I think you bought some, but I don't give a shit about chilies. I want you to talk to me."

I couldn't remember if I bought chilies or not, but I always forgot what I bought even before I started to lose my mind. Sighing, Scott rummaged through the produce drawer in the refrigerator and placed the chilies on the counter.

"Here," he said. "I'll help you since you're not talking. You want them diced or what?"

"Yeah, I think so," I said.

"What do you mean *you think so*? Do you or don't you? I can just slice them or —"

"Just shut the fuck up, Scott." Stunned and embarrassed with myself, I stared down at the kitchen counter, also wondering where I put the strainer to rinse the chickpeas. I felt Scott's eyes on me, as shocked as I was. My mind blanked again. "Fuck," I muttered.

"What's wrong?" His tone was softer, no longer annoyed. "Something's wrong, and you're not telling me. What is it, Terry?"

My eyes teared, contemplating what to say. I didn't want Scott to think I was unfaithful. "I got lost," I finally told him.

"That's not a big deal. Why didn't you tell me that in the first place? Where'd you go?"

"Downtown," I answered.

"What do you mean you got lost downtown?" he laughed. It wasn't funny because it was real. "You go there all the time. Where'd you go? Really?"

"I couldn't find Millie's. That's why I didn't get Paul his ice cream."

"I don't understand. How could you get lost? Did you have a couple of beers and a few shots of tequila or something? If you did, you should have invited me. I needed a break."

"No. I'm being serious, Scott. I totally blanked. It was fucking scary and you're laughing like this is a joke. It's not a fucking joke." I took the chili from him because he was doing it all wrong.

"I'm not laughing. Maybe you're stressed about something. Sometimes when I'm driving I can't remember how I got there. I just zone out."

"I wasn't driving." I stopped chopping and looked at him. "I think I might have a brain tumor or something."

"You don't have a brain tumor," Scott said. "Stop it."

"How do you know? I forget things all the time, and it's getting worse."

"Maybe you're not getting enough sleep. You're being paranoid."

"Fuck, Scott. I'm fucking losing my mind, and you're giving me false reassurances." Not one to swear, I found myself out of control tonight.

"I'm sorry," Scott said. "If you're that worried, you should see your doctor."

"You don't believe me. You think I'm lying and cheating on you. What a fucking great marriage we have, huh? You don't fucking trust me. How long have we been together, anyway?"

We had been together for twenty-six years, and I had hoped to be together for another twenty-six, even though we had our differences. Every couple had their differences, but we always made up. We had one rule: never go to bed angry... and we never did.

"Stop, Terry." Scott squeezed my arm. With his free hand, he took the knife from me. "I believe you. I can see you're not yourself. I have to tell you, I'm really worried."

"Are you guys okay?" Paul called to us from the other room.

"Yeah, everything's fine," I replied, sitting down at the kitchen table. "You're right; I'm not myself. I... I... I feel so lost. I honestly didn't know where I was, and my memory is... well, it's getting worse. I don't think I have a brain tumor. I'm not depressed or anxious, and I get plenty of sleep. I've been ignoring it because I didn't want it to be true, but I can't ignore it anymore because it's happening."

"What's happening?" Scott asked, sitting beside me.

I didn't want to say it or admit it, but the time had come. "My mother had Alzheimer's, remember? And I may have it, too."

"You're only fifty-six. How could you have Alzheimer's?"

"It could be early onset. My mother was diagnosed at sixty-two, but she had symptoms in her fifties. I didn't recognize it at the time."

"How long has this been going on?" he asked.

"A while. I use my phone to compensate, and I write everything down. I have sticky notes everywhere. You didn't notice?"

"No, I noticed. It was easier for me to think you were having an affair."

"I'd never cheat on you. You know that, right?"

"Yes. Just be honest with me next time so I don't freak out on you. Promise me, Terry. If it is what you think it is, you shouldn't go through this alone. I'm here for you." His words reminded me that he loved me unconditionally, and I couldn't bear the thought of leaving him.

I never had a reason to see a doctor, except for my annual physical. Scott and I were active and physically fit. Scott had bouts of anxiety and depression, but we worked through it together as a family.

After a thorough medical exam and several appointments with more blood work than I'd ever had before, followed by an MRI and a CT-scan, my primary care physician referred me to a neuropsychologist. Other than my failing memory, I was healthy. The neuropsychologist, Dr. Nasser, performed a series of cognitive tests, a bunch of stupid questions that exhausted me. I just wanted to go home and sleep and not have a lengthy conversation with Scott. I couldn't even remember what questions Dr. Nasser asked me. I didn't want to go back to her office for her to remind me of how poorly I did, but Scott insisted we go.

As I zoned out, wondering what to make for dinner, Scott asked question after question. He had various excuses why I did poorly on the tests, so poorly I walked out of the office with a diagnosis of Alzheimer's disease, scoring in the mild to moderate range.

"Scott," I interrupted him, heading to a car I wasn't sure was ours. "I wasn't tired, and I wasn't depressed or anxious. It is what it is."

"I hate that expression," he said.

"But it's the truth. We can't change the truth. In a couple of years, you're going to resent me. You're going to wish you never made that midnight trip to Vermont."

In the middle of the parking lot, Scott stopped me, clutching my wrist. "That won't ever happen," he said. "I won't ever let you go. I have no regrets and that won't ever change. Our car's over there." He held my arm, guiding me in the right direction.

Whenever Scott was worried or anxious, he talked incessantly. As he drove home, I let him rant, frequently changing subjects, always ending up with me, assuring me that "everything would be okay," even though "everything" wouldn't be "okay." He continued to talk as we entered the empty house. At one in the afternoon, Paul was still at school.

"I don't want to talk anymore," I said. "My head hurts."

"Why don't you lie down?" he said. "I should get to work, anyway. I have a lot to do and—"

I cut him off, hugging him. I didn't want him to work. I just wanted to hug him forever and continue to tell me everything was going to be okay even if it wasn't.

"Maybe I won't work," he said. "I'm not in the mood to work, anyway."

Although it was only one in the afternoon, we went to bed together. At least I didn't forget how to make love. I had read somewhere that libido and the taste of chocolate were the last things to go.

* * *

At night, I lay awake, staring at the calendar on the wall. I circled tomorrow, the day when Ariel and Luna were coming home for Easter break. Scott and I discussed breaking the news to everyone at the same time. I propped myself up on my elbow, facing Scott as he slept on his side, one arm over my stomach. Still as handsome as the first day I met him, his hair just as dark with specks of gray scattered here and there, like his father, his eyes often spoke a thousand words.

There were a lot of things I wanted to tell him, but I couldn't remember what. I had been writing things down more and more, but I had misplaced my mini notepad.

"I hate it when you watch me sleep," he mumbled. "What time is it?"

"Two in the morning," I replied, bringing my hand to the side of his head. "Scott, I have to tell you something." I thought my hardest, trying to remember what I intended to tell him. "I love you," I said, although I wasn't too sure that's what I wanted to say, but it felt like the right thing to say because I meant it.

"I love you, too," he said, leaning over to kiss me. As we kissed, he rolled on top of me. "I wish it was me instead of you. You made me the man I am today."

I wrapped my arms around him, enjoying his kisses, anticipating more since he always gave more. Tonight was no different.

As a tight-knit family, Ariel and Luna never strayed too far from home, each attending college in Vermont. One of them always came home every other weekend. I never complained. They were also perceptive and sensed the tension in the air, especially as me and Scott glanced at each other uneasily, searching for the right moment.

"Something's weird," Luna said. "Dad, you've barely said a word all night."

"I have to tell you guys something," I finally said.

"You're finally divorcing Papi," Ariel joked. "He's finally made you lose your mind."

Scott took a sip of his water, looking away from everyone, not amused.

"Shut up, Ariel," Luna said. "I think something's really wrong. You guys aren't really breaking up, are you?"

"Why does everyone think this has to do with me and Papi?" I said. "We're not splitting up. He may think differently in a couple of years."

Scott turned to me, glaring at me. "We're not breaking up," Scott said. "We're fine. I'll never think differently."

"Then what's going on?" Luna asked.

"I've been diagnosed with Alzheimer's disease," I finally said. "My mother had it, and now I have it."

"You're kidding," Ariel said.

"Does it look like he's kidding?" Luna said. "Why would he joke about something like this?"

"What's Alzheimer's?" Paul asked.

"It's a progressive neurological disease," Scott explained, as if a twelve-year-old would understand what that meant.

"It's a brain disease," I clarified. "It affects your memory, so I can't remember some things. Progressive means it will only get worse, and there's no cure."

"I don't get it. Isn't that what old people get?" Luna said.

"I'm old," I stated.

"No, you're not," Ariel said. "You're not even sixty. Are you sure?"

"I've been poked and prodded and had tons of tests and a cognitive assessment," I said. "You name it, I had it."

"Are you going to die?" Paul asked.

"We're all going to die someday," I said.

"That's not what Paul meant, and you know it," Ariel said.

"Don't worry," I assured everyone. "I feel fine. Just forgetful. I have strategies that help me. Anyway, I may live another fifteen to twenty years, driving you all crazy."

I laughed, but no one else did. Both my parents died in their sixties.

As far as I knew, no Lachance lived to be seventy, but longevity ran in Scott's family. His parents were in their mid-eighties and going strong.

"Maybe they'll find a cure soon," Luna said. She was always so upbeat and optimistic. She'd make a great counselor some day.

I could only hope.

27

Chapter 27

2017

Scott

Terry hadn't spoken to me all week, not since I took away his car keys after the police caught him driving the wrong way on the highway. Fortunately, it was the middle of the night, so the highway was empty. I had previously told him not to drive at night, but for some reason he felt the need to go for a ride at three in the morning while I was fast asleep. He couldn't tell me where he was going or why. He was lucky the police only gave him a warning after I told them about his condition. That's when they advised me to take away the keys. In fact, I gave away the car and I hid my keys, which also annoyed him.

According to Terry, everyone was lying, that he never did what the police claimed he did, that he would never drive the wrong way on the highway. Terry swore he'd never forgive me. Instead of having one teenager in the house, I felt like I had two.

His moods fluctuated so much, I could never predict what he was going to say or do. One minute he was depressed and withdrawn, the next minute he was the Terry Lachance we all knew. Other times, he bounced from one subject to the next and sometimes wandered around the house with no destination. Once he recognized he was wandering aimlessly, he'd become depressed and withdrawn again. He waited until Paul left for school to lay it on me, airing his grievances about me, himself, and everything else that popped into his head. At the kitchen table, he barely touched his oatmeal, convinced he had already eaten breakfast. In reality, he had eaten nothing since last night.

"I hope I have a heart attack and die instantly," he said to me.

"Oh, you're talking to me again," I said. "Well, I hope you don't have a heart attack and die instantly because I'm not ready to say goodbye to you."

Terry was always optimistic, the one who wanted to save the world, rarely ever depressed or anxious. Over the last two years, his worldview had changed drastically.

"Everyday I lose more of myself," he said. "You'll wish I had a heart attack and died instantly, too, when I don't recognize you or our kids, when I forget how to eat, walk, and speak. I don't want to put you through that. I've put you through enough. Trust me, you'll wish I was dead. I hated seeing my mother like that, and that's what's going to happen to me. It's coming."

"I'll always be there for you," I said. "I won't let you go."

"Fuck you." He stormed off, running up the stairs. *What did I do now?*

"Terry!" I shouted, worried he'd do something to himself. I found him in our room, sitting on the edge of the bed, gripping the sheets.

"I don't want you to be there for me," he said. "I want you to let me go. You know what I really want? A fucking bullet to my head. I can't handle this, Scott. Just fucking shoot me. Soon I'll be wetting the bed, and you'll be changing my diapers like I'm a baby. I don't want that, Scott."

Sometimes he couldn't find the bathroom, so Paul made signs all over the house, hoping that would prevent him from urinating in the trash can. If I showed an ounce of worry or concern, then Terry would shut down and sink into an even deeper depression, feeling guilty and ashamed.

"Don't even think about shooting yourself," I said, crouching in front of him, forcing him to look at me. "Don't let me find you somewhere with your brains splattered everywhere. You've never been selfish. Don't start now."

"Don't worry. I'm not going to put a bullet in my head. We don't even own a gun. The best thing would be for me to die in my sleep, and I hope it's soon."

I sat beside him, not sure how to help him. Imagining my life without him was too painful. We'd been together for twenty-eight years and never spent one night apart. We were aiming for thirty years.

"I won't ever let you go," I said. "You mean too much to me."

"I don't want to hear that, Scott. Maybe the time isn't right, but when it is, I want you to let me go. I know it'll be hard for you, but I'm begging you, Scott, when I don't recognize myself in the mirror, when I don't recognize you or our kids, when I can't walk... " His eyes filled with water, his voice shaking. "When I can't eat... just let me go, okay? I don't want any feeding tubes or machines or anything like that to keep me alive. By that point, my brain is already gone. Do you understand?"

"Yes," I said, squeezing his hand. He had talked about his end of life wishes at least a dozen times. "I'll do whatever you want." He leaned into me, sobbing against my shoulder. I brought my arm around him, holding him close to me. "But today you know who you are and who we are, and we have Ariel's wedding coming up. You don't want to miss it, do you?"

Ariel and his long-time girlfriend, Jill, planned on marrying in three months at the Inn and Cottages where Terry was most familiar and comfortable.

"You're Ariel's best man, remember?" I immediately regretted using the word remember. "I'm sorry, Terry. I didn't..."

"I remember," he said. "Ariel would be disappointed if I wasn't there. Are a lot of people coming?"

"No," I replied. Ariel and Jill only wanted a small wedding, no more than forty people. Large crowds overwhelmed Terry.

"Okay. I'll be there," he said.

"Good." I kissed the side of his head. "I love you. I'll always be there for you. I promise to carry out your wishes."

"I believe you," he said. "You've been an amazing partner. I don't have any regrets, do you?"

"No. None."

"I'm sorry, Scott. I don't want to leave you."

"You're not leaving me," I said, fighting back my own tears. "You'll always be with me."

"When my mom got sick, I had just gotten back from El Salvador. She was so forgetful, much like I am now. I remember asking her what if you forget me? How could a mother forget her only child? She looked at me and said, 'love never forgets.' In her final days, when she couldn't speak, the way she looked at me, I knew she was right. There were days, too, when her eyes said nothing. They were vacant and hollow, but you get the idea. When that happens to me, remember that, okay? When I can't speak, remember I still love you because love never forgets."

"Yeah... okay," I said, swallowing hard. "Love never forgets. I'll remember that."

"I'm upsetting you. Sorry about that."

"I'd rather you talk about it than keep it all inside. It's okay to be angry."

"Yeah, I'm more than angry. I'm really going to miss you, Scott."

"You're still here," I said, hugging him tightly. "I'm not ready to let you go yet. There's so much more to do. Now will you please come back downstairs and have breakfast? You'll feel better after you eat something."

"Yeah, okay. I'm kinda hungry, I guess."

By the time we returned to the kitchen, Terry had forgotten about the conversation we just had in the bedroom, all except for one thing. As I placed a fresh bowl of hot oatmeal in front of him, Terry looked at me and repeated something he said upstairs.

"Love never forgets."

* * *

In the bathroom longer than usual, Terry stood there, still in his pajamas, holding his toothbrush, acting as though the toothbrush was a foreign object. If we didn't hurry up, we were going to be late for our own son's wedding.

"Hey, Terry, what are you doing?" I asked, peeking in the bathroom. Terry wasn't even close to being ready while I was shaved, showered, and dressed. "We're going to be late."

"I... um... where are we going?" he asked.

"To Ariel's wedding," I said, doing my best to disguise my frustration. We didn't have time to waste. To move him along, I squeezed some toothpaste on his toothbrush.

"You look nice," he said as I closed the bathroom door. "Why are you wearing a tuxedo?"

"For Ariel and Jill's wedding." Taking a deep breath, I held back my anger and annoyance. *This isn't Terry's fault*, I told myself. There was a lot going on, and I just wanted everything to go smoothly for Ariel and Jill. "Come on, Terry, brush your teeth. You still have to take a shower."

As he stared blankly at me, I realized he didn't know what to do with the toothbrush. After I guided it to his mouth, he completed the task. Stumped with what to do next, he waited for my instruction. "Are you taking a shower with me?" he asked as I lifted his pajama top over his head.

"No. There's no time for that."

"What are we doing?"

"*You* are taking a shower," I said. "So get in." I did everything for him, from washing his hair, to drying him off. He insisted on shaving himself, but I kept a close eye on him so he wouldn't hurt himself.

"Scott," he said as I buttoned up his shirt. Buttons proved to be Terry's arch-nemesis.

"Yeah?"

"I love you," he said out of the blue, causing me to slow down.

"I love you, too."

"Thank you for helping me."

"Yeah, no problem." I helped him into his top coat. "It's like going to the prom, huh? Oh, wait, you didn't go. Well, you didn't miss much."

"You look nice," he said again. "Did I tell you that already?"

"Yeah, but I don't mind hearing it again."

"Do you ever wish you married a woman?"

"What?" I laughed, now working on his bow tie. "No way. Why would I want to marry anyone else but you, anyway?"

"We've had a lot of fun together, haven't we?"

"Yes," I said, placing a hand on his shoulders, admiring his eyes that sparkled this morning. "I always thought you were so handsome. You still are."

He held the side of my face and brought his lips to mine. I loved it when he turned into that twenty-year-old Terry. If we didn't have the wedding in an hour, I would have taken him back to our bedroom.

At the reception, Terry masked his memory deficits by smiling, dancing, and staying by my side all afternoon. Only people who really knew him spotted a difference. In the past, he'd usually initiate conversation with either Mike or my parents but not today. He stuck to me most of the day, relying on me to protect him and keep him safe.

He only left my side to dance with the bride. Music relaxed him. While sitting with Mike, Michelle, and my parents, I watched Terry dance, smiling and enjoying himself.

"How are you doing?" Mike asked me.

"Okay," I lied, taking my eyes off Terry for a second. In reality, I was about to fall apart.

"No, you're not," Mike said. "I can see a difference in him."

"Yeah." I swallowed my tears. "He's slipping away. It's progressing faster than I expected. It's heart-breaking. It's really fucking heart-breaking. A few months ago, Terry wished for a bullet in his head, and I have to admit, sometimes I don't think that would be such a bad thing. I can't even believe I'm saying that." I took a large sip of my wine. "He's suffering, and I don't want to see him suffer."

"He doesn't look like he's suffering," Mike said as Terry looked in my direction, smiling. "I can see you're taking good care of him. He looks happy."

"Today he is," I said as Terry broke away from Jill who then turned to Ariel.

As he approached me, Terry reached for my hand. With my hand in his, he led me to the dance floor. "You were always a great dancer," he said as I took the lead.

"You're not bad, either," I said.

"I learned from the best."

Everything went as planned. Ariel and Jill hadn't been happier, and Terry beamed with pride all day. Terry and I danced most of the night, even when my legs were about to give out. Terry didn't want to stop. If he stopped, then he'd remember he couldn't remember. As Dr. Nasser said, he was at the point when "he knew he didn't know," and that's what bothered him the most. However, despite everything he said, he wasn't ready to go yet.

28

Chapter 28

2018

Scott

For the third time in a month, the police found Terry wandering the streets at night, looking for something he couldn't recall. The double locks and bolts on the doors of our house failed yet again. He couldn't remember how to tie his shoes, but he could undo the locks. He never knew where he was going.

"Papi, where are you going?" fifteen-year-old Paul asked, standing in the hallway.

"Your dad got lost again," I said, running down the stairs, Paul not far behind me. I imagined Terry scared to death, as always.

"How?" Paul said. "You double bolted the doors."

"He's like Houdini. Stay here. I'll be back."

This time the police dropped him off at the nearest hospital instead of holding him at the police station. He waited for me in the emergency room, pacing back and forth, a security guard monitoring him closely. Before going to bed, Terry had refused to change into his pajamas for whatever reason. I had to pick my battles and figured there were worse things than going to bed in sweatpants and a hoodie. Well-nourished, physically fit, and overall put together for someone who needed help with everything except walking and eating, he could have passed as a hospital visitor and looked normal until he spoke. Sometimes he had a hard time finding the right words, and other times he couldn't find the words at all. Sometimes he knew the year; other times he didn't have a clue. Sometimes he didn't know my name, but he recognized me and our kids. Sometimes he made love like he was twenty again.

"What am I doing here?" Terry asked me as I approached him. "I don't know where I am. Where am I?"

"You're at Saint Joseph's Hospital," I answered.

"Oh, yeah, I'm in a hospital," he said, his eyes wandering around the emergency room. "Why? Am I sick?"

I didn't quite know how to answer that since technically he was sick, but he didn't look sick. Six months ago, his doctor recommended we get a medical alert bracelet with my name and phone number inscribed on it. Terry promised he would never take it off, but his promises didn't always mean anything because he'd often forget he made the promise in the first place.

"Where's Paul?" he asked.

"At home."

"How could you leave him alone?"

"He's fifteen," I reminded him.

"Oh, yeah, that's right. They're not going to lock me up, are they?" Terry asked, his eyes scanning the emergency room suspiciously, paranoid someone would stick him in handcuffs or a straight jacket, afraid the police would lock him up in prison, and he'd never see me again. He imagined scenes from *The Snake Pit* or *One Flew Over the Cuckoo's Nest*. So far I had kept him out of a psych unit. "Don't let them lock me up."

"I won't ever let anyone lock you up," I said. "Come on, let's go home."

He clenched my hand as I walked him out of the hospital and to the car. As he shuffled through the parking lot, I realized he was wearing his slippers. I didn't say anything, hoping he wouldn't fall on our way to the car. He had a tendency to trip over his feet.

At two in the morning, Paul sat at the kitchen with his phone, texting someone frantically, no doubt his twenty-seven-year-old brother, Ariel, and twenty-three-year-old sister, Luna.

"Dad, where'd you go?" Paul asked.

"It's late," I said. "You should be in bed."

"Go to bed," Terry said, wandering off.

"Papi, he's going the wrong way again," Paul said as Terry headed into the living room. Our bedroom was upstairs.

"Yeah, we'll talk in the morning," I said.

The next step was to install door and bed alarms that would alert me any time Terry got up in the middle of the night. I also got him an ankle bracelet that went off whenever he left the house unattended. In his younger days, Terry was always a good sleeper but not anymore. Now he slept for three to four hours a night and intermittently slept during the day. His confusion came at night with periods of lucidity during the day. I hadn't had a good night's sleep in two years. I was only fifty-six and stuck babysitting my fifty-eight-year-old husband.

That's not to say I didn't love him. I adored him and promised to love him in sickness and in health, and I didn't want to break that promise. But what about my health? On the brink of insanity and at risk of resenting the man I loved so much, I occasionally considered placing him in a locked unit in a nursing home to keep him safe. But guilt prevented me from doing it. I couldn't picture him living in a nursing home with eighty-year-old men and women.

The next day, after picking Terry up at the emergency room, I called our contractor to install alarms on every door of the house, including our bedroom. Terry watched the two strange men's every move. I hoped he wouldn't suddenly freak out and kick them out of the house. To him, they were strange men, but in reality we had been using these contractors for years. They built the extension to our house. Terry insisted he had never seen them before.

"Ivy's coming soon," I said, attempting to distract him. Ivy, a forty-eight-year-old mother of two teenage boys, had been one of Terry's caregivers for the past three months. She was more like a babysitter because I couldn't watch him twenty-four hours a day, and I didn't expect Paul to do it. Luna and Ariel lived nearby in their own apartments and helped as much as they could. Luna contemplated moving back home to "save money," she said, but I sensed guilt played a part in her decision-making.

"You like Ivy, right?" I said.

"Ivy... yeah... yeah," Terry said. The tone of his voice indicated he didn't remember her name. He'd most likely remember once he saw her. "Why do I have to wear this?" he asked as I attached a bracelet to his ankle.

"Sometimes you get confused at night. The police keep picking you up on the streets."

"No, they don't," he insisted. By nature, Terry wasn't argumentative, but things were different these days. "Who says I'm confused? You want to keep me prisoner here in my own house."

"That's not what I want." I counted the minutes before Ivy's arrival.

"I'm taking this fucking thing off."

Not in the mood to argue with him, I walked away, leaving him alone in the living room by the front door to supervise our contractors, whom he continued to claim he'd never met. In a few minutes, I expected him in my office, having forgotten he was angry. He also forgot all about the bracelet on his ankle.

"Are you mad at me?" he asked as I was about to sit down at my desk.

"No," I said.

"Did I do something wrong?"

"No."

"Why do I feel like I did?" He was in one of those moods, a combination of depression, anger, and lucidity. Instead of sitting down at my desk, I went to him. A kiss and a hug usually helped. The Lachances were always the hugging-type.

"Come on, let's get something to eat," I said, walking him out of the office and into the kitchen. A slice of chocolate cake also did the trick.

29

Chapter 29

2019

Scott

Exhausted after a busy night of wandering in and out of the bedroom and up and down the stairs, Terry sat in his favorite rocking chair in the living room, facing the over-sized bay windows overlooking the still, quiet lake.

As a freelance graphic designer, I had accumulated a decent amount of clients over the years. My income helped put Ariel and Luna through college. Luna now assisted Angie in running the camp while earning a Master's degree in counseling. Incapable of running a business anymore, Terry relied on me to keep the place going. I was always a silent co-owner. Two years ago, I hired a manager, someone Terry and I knew well and trusted, to run the place.

Swamped with tons of work and pending projects, I didn't know how I was going to get it all done. Ivy, Terry's dedicated caregiver, showed up with a terrible cold, so I sent her home. The last thing Terry needed was a cold or something worse.

Last month he spent three days in the hospital with pneumonia.

Strange, unfamiliar places frightened him, so he begged me to take him home. Doctors told me that Terry was aspirating on either his saliva, food, liquid, or all three, causing aspiration pneumonia. A speech therapist suggested thickening his liquids with something called Thick-it, which would help with his swallowing difficulties, but Terry wanted nothing to do with that. He refused to drink anything with that "shit in it," he said. In the end, I just wanted him to be happy. If an ice cream cone, pint of beer, or a Coke made him happy, then I'd give it to him, aware of the risks involved.

Terry didn't always recognize Ivy, which both frightened and annoyed him. Whenever Paul and I weren't around, he asked for us incessantly. At sixteen, Paul should have been more focused on school and sports, his favorite pastime, but he gave up sports to help care for his dad. Paul would do anything for him. Strong-willed with a good head on his shoulders, Paul ignored me when I told him not to quit soccer.

I desperately needed a nap but couldn't afford to take a break, not even when Paul came home from school. Calm at the moment, Terry rocked slowly back and forth.

"Someone's having a baby," he said as I sat on an armchair beside him, my eyes focused on my laptop. He forgot most things, but he remembered someone close to us was having a baby.

"Yes," I said. "Our son, Ariel, is having a baby."

"When?" he asked.

"In two months."

"Two months," he repeated, closing his eyes.

When Terry was in the right mood, we'd listen to music and dance. Dancing kept us connected, and even though he didn't always remember my name, he knew me. I was the person who made him feel safe. I was the man who loved him more than anyone else.

However, sometimes I found myself resenting the man I loved. I resented him because I was healthy and relatively young and couldn't live my own life because he freaked out every time I left the house. I resented him because he left me, through no fault of his own, yet I saw him every day, a shell of a man he once was.

But I still adored him and couldn't imagine sleeping in another bed in the house, as our kids suggested. I was his other half, and he knew it. Besides, I didn't trust him sleeping in another bed by himself in another room.

At two-thirty in the afternoon, Paul dropped his school bag at the front door and went directly to Terry. "Hi, Dad."

Terry didn't respond, merely glancing at him. He dozed on and off all day while I sat in a chair beside him, attempting to work.

"He didn't sleep again, huh?" Paul said. "And neither did you. Where's Ivy?"

"I sent her home," I said. "She's sick. I really have to get some work done. Could you watch him for a few hours?"

"Yeah, sure," Paul replied.

Eager to get the hell out of there, I kissed Terry's cheek and headed to the door. "Wait!" Terry shouted to me. "Where are you going?"

"I'll be back in a few minutes," I said.

Time meant nothing to Terry. He didn't know the difference between a few minutes or a few hours. "Where are you going?" he asked again.

"To get some coffee. I'll bring you back some."

Satisfied with my response, he returned to staring out the window.

"Call me if you need anything," I said to Paul. "I'll just be at the coffee shop downtown."

As I rested my elbows on a table in the coffee shop, I broke down, bawling into my hands, too tired and emotionally drained to work, too busy feeling sorry for myself.

A part of me wanted it all to be over, for Terry to go to sleep and never wake up. What kind of person was I to wish that on anybody, especially the man I loved? Another part of me wanted to hang on to him forever, not something Terry wanted. One of the regular girls placed a hot mocha latte in front of me. "It's on the house."

"Thanks," I said, attempting to regain my composure.

Because Terry and I had been coming here for years, the staff knew us well. Terry had been a regular in the town since he was a boy, always well-liked. There was nothing not to like about him. He had an ability to make everyone feel good and welcomed.

After a much needed mocha latte, I was able to focus and get some work done with no calls or text messages from Paul. That was a good thing.

When I returned home, I found Paul sitting in Terry's chair, but I didn't see Terry. He needed constant supervision, which Paul didn't always understand. "Where's your dad?" I asked, on the verge of panicking.

"He's outside," Paul said matter-of-factly. "He didn't want to be inside. He's fine."

From the window, I observed Terry walking by the lake, a few people fishing not far away but still far enough that they wouldn't be able to save him if he floundered in the water. In May, the water was too cold to swim in.

"He's not fine," I said, running outside to get him. In denial at times, Paul sometimes believed Terry wasn't as impaired as he really was.

"Maybe he just wants to go swimming," Paul said, trailing behind me.

"He can't remember how to swim," I said to Paul, grabbing Terry's arm. "Besides, the water's too cold. You can't ever leave him alone, not even when you're watching him from the window. All you have to do is turn your head for a minute and he could be gone, face-down in the lake, dead."

"Okay," he said defensively. "I won't do it again. You overreact about everything."

"I'm not overreacting." As I led him inside, Terry stopped walking, refusing to go any farther.

"I'm sorry I got angry," I said to both Paul and Terry. "I'm just a little stressed right now. Do you want to go for a ride in the boat?" I asked Terry. "I'll row, although I suck at it."

"Okay," Terry said. It was an unusually warm early evening in May. I understood why Terry didn't want to be inside.

"Are you sure?" Paul asked me. "You look kinda tired."

"I'm okay," I said, watching Terry's eyes shift to the rowboats, canoes, and kayaks. He really wanted to go out on the boat. "Come on." I hooked my arm around Terry's.

Down by the boats, I fetched a life preserver. Terry was always a great swimmer, but now I wasn't so sure. I assumed he forgot how to swim. "Why do I need to wear this?" he asked as I helped him into the life preserver.

"Because I don't want you to drown," I answered.

"How come you're not wearing one?"

"Because I can swim."

"So can I."

"Well, sometimes you forget. Let's just go, huh?"

I rowed to our spot, somewhere we hadn't been in a long time. He jumped out of the boat before I docked it. "I remember this place!"

"Slow down!" I shouted to him as he ran off.

He unzipped his life preserver and dropped it on the ground. As if he were still twenty, he stripped naked and swung from the rope, landing in the cold water. There was no stopping him. Afraid he'd drown, I immediately jumped in after him, shrieking as my body hit the cold water. Terry burst into laughter, laughing at me, like old times.

Tonight was different. Tonight he swam well, almost like his old self. As his laughter subsided, he swam up to me and kissed me, kissing me long and hard. I fought back my tears, staying in the moment, responding to his kisses. This place must have done something for him, triggering many memories.

"You're cold," he said as I shivered in his arms. Although his body shook, he denied being cold.

"Yes, I'm freezing," I said through chattering teeth.

"Let's get out then." He walked toward the boat, forgetting about his clothes.

"Hey, Terry, wait!" As I gathered up his clothes, he did as I said, waiting for me by the boat.

"Scott, I want you to do something for me," he said as I helped him get dressed. My eyes teared as he said my name since he rarely said it these days. "I want you to let me go. If you love me, you'll let me go."

Not this again, I thought to myself. He'd been telling me this for years.

"Where are you going?" I asked with a nervous laugh.

"I just want to go."

"I don't think it's your time. Do you know you're as handsome as the first day I met you?" I said to distract him, more to distract me. "I loved the way your hair flopped over your eyes. It drove me wild."

"You're not listening to me, Scott. It's not your time. It's not... not... it's not... um... well, our son, Pau..." Paul's name was on the tip of his tongue.

"Paul," I said.

"It's not Paul's time."

"He's your son, and you're his dad. It's never going to be the right time for him. What do you want me to do, anyway? Kill you? Euthanasia's not legal, you know. Anyway, you promised you'd stick around until our grandchild is born. You want to find out if it's a boy or girl, right?"

"Shit, I forgot. Of course I'll be here. How much longer?"

"Two months."

"Okay," he sighed. "I like this place. We've been here before."

“Yeah, a few times.”

As I rowed, Terry lay back in the boat, dozing off. Every once in a while, I’d kick his leg because I didn’t want him falling asleep. I figured if I tired him out, he’d get some sleep tonight. He hummed an unrecognizable song, my arms shaking from the cold.

Paul was there by the lake, waiting for us. “What happened to you?” he asked me.

“We went for a swim,” I replied. “Can you dock the boat? I need to get out of these clothes.”

“Yeah, sure,” Paul said.

I needed a nice, hot shower and hoped Terry would come with me. Getting him in the shower these days was a challenge. Despite the increased confusion he experienced later in the day, tonight he was clearer than he had been in a long time. As he hugged me, warm water beat down on my back as he rested his chin on my shoulder. I realized I couldn’t let him go, not if we continued to have moments like this. I wasn’t ready to say goodbye.

30

Chapter 30

2020

Scott

Within a month, Terry fell ten times. Each time he fell, I had to physically pick him up because he couldn't get up on his own. He shuffled when he walked, often stumbling over his own feet. One of these days I feared he'd fall down the stairs and break a hip or crack his head open. Worse than ever, he wandered the house day and night, barely taking breaks to sit and rest.

This morning I woke to a loud thud that shook the house. I ran to the bathroom, finding Terry lying on the hard, cold floor in a puddle of urine. He tried to make it to the bathroom in time, but he didn't make it... again.

"I... I..." he stammered, struggling more and more these days with finding the right words. Sometimes he'd go days without saying a word.

"It's okay," I assured him.

Once again, he was lucky he didn't break a bone. Because his face bounced against the toilet, he'd end up with a black eye or a black and blue forehead. Together, Paul and I lifted Terry to his feet. At six in the morning, I was about to pass out from exhaustion.

"I'll clean him up," Paul said. Unlike me, Paul could always get Terry into the shower. He had a kind, calm, and patient way with him. My patience had long run out. Sometimes Terry would lash out at me, swatting at me or throwing punches. He mostly lashed out when he was scared and frustrated, like when he didn't understand what I asked him to do. Paul never gave him any options, telling him what to do. Terry seemed to do whatever he said.

As I made my way to the kitchen, I overheard music coming from a phone upstairs. From the kitchen, I heard Terry sing *The Boxer*. He could still sing the entire song from memory.

After making a cup of coffee, I went to the office and dug out the manila folder where we stored our legal documents. He and I had gone through them together several times when he was with it and able to make his own decisions. He outlined everything he wanted—or didn't want—as his illness progressed. As I opened the folder, I discovered a handwritten letter Terry slipped in there without me knowing. I sat at the desk, reading the letter while Paul showered him upstairs.

February 15, 2017

Hi Scott,

If you found this letter, then it means I'm no longer lucid. I bet you're looking for the answers you already know, a reassurance. You're here because I'm still here but only in body. I'm sorry.

Thank you for your support throughout this whole ordeal. We both knew there would come a time when you'd have to make some difficult decisions and, as always, I trust you'll make the right ones. The time is now.

I do not want you, Scott, my husband, lover, and best friend, to be my caregiver. I want you to remain my husband and best friend and to remember me as your lover. I do not want to be your patient. I do not want to be someone you'll grow to resent.

As much as I'd like to stay home with you and Paul at the place where I've lived all of my life, I understand that this may not be feasible. Don't feel bad about it. When I become incontinent and can't eat and drink on my own and when I can't walk, I give you permission to place me in a nursing home. Never feel bad about it.

Scott, as we've discussed many times, I do not want any heroic means to keep me alive. That means no feeding tubes or IVs, no CPR if my heart stops, no breathing tubes, no hospitalizations, and you know the rest. Just let me go.

Never feel guilty for doing what you have to do. You're amazing, and I'll always love you. I'll always love Ariel, Luna, and Paul. We've lived an incredible life. Remember to take care of yourself, too. I love you so much. I know we'll meet again someday.

All my love,

Terry

In my head, I heard Terry's voice reading the letter over and over.

"Papi?" Paul startled me. I closed the folder, quickly brushing away my tears.

"Yeah?" I said, sniffing. "How's your dad?"

"He's sitting in bed, looking at his phone. Are you okay?"

"Yeah, I'm fine. Luna and Ariel are coming over later. I think we all have to talk." Taking a deep breath, I returned to my bedroom.

With his phone in his hand, Terry looked down at a picture of our nine-month-old granddaughter. He enjoyed looking at photos, particularly old ones of the two of us. I sat beside him, assisting him in scrolling through the photos. "What's her name?" he asked, staring down at the photo of the baby.

"Terry," I said.

"I like that name."

"It's your name," I reminded him. "Ariel and Jill named her after you. It's one of those names that can go either way, boy or girl."

"Oh," he said. "She's a beautiful baby."

"Yes, she is. You love holding her."

Whenever he held the baby, he reverted to the Terry we all knew and loved, at least for a few fleeting minutes.

I got up and retrieved the memory book Luna made for him a few months ago. She even included baby pictures of himself. He agreed that he was a cute baby. "I know him," he said, stopping at a picture of me back in 1992. Up on water skis, Terry surprised me by snapping a Polaroid, causing me to fall face first in the water. I could still hear his laughter in my head.

"Yeah, it's me," I said. "I have a lot more gray now." I took after my dad with a mixture of dark hair with specks of gray. Terry's hair turned a very light shade of brown, just as I remembered his dad. Terry looked at me and half-smiled, then returned to the photos, turning the page.

"I like this one," he said, referring to a photo taken of the two of us at Mike's wedding. Slightly inebriated, Terry draped his arm over my shoulder, the two of us smiling broadly.

"See how handsome you were?" I said. "You still are."

"That's me and you?"

"Yes." This book had an amazing effect on Terry, triggering many memories. "We got so drunk. It was those damn tequila shots. I never learned."

"Yeah," he said with an even bigger smile, as if he understood what I was talking about.

Terry absolutely loved this book, spending hours looking at it. He and I would sit together as I reminded him who each person was. He'd then point out his favorite photos. This book became his greatest possession, and I enjoyed looking through it with him.

As usual, he barely ate any breakfast. He didn't know what to do with the eating utensils, and he didn't want anyone feeding him. Because of his lack of appetite and food refusals, he continued to lose weight, having lost ten pounds in a month. He didn't weigh more than a hundred and ten pounds.

With a piece of raisin toast, he went to his rocking chair where he sat for ten minutes before wandering around the first floor of the house. In the summer, the Inn and Cottages swarmed with people, so Ivy would take him for walks off the property, away from the crowds. With the onset of COVID-19, we weren't sure what this summer had in store for the camp or the Inn. Since Paul attended school remotely, he was a big help around the house.

While Terry, Paul, Ariel, Luna, and I sat in the living room, Jill sat in a chair beside Terry in the rocking chair, letting him hold his granddaughter. I planned on discussing how we planned on caring for their dad as he continued to deteriorate. As much as I hated the idea, I was about to bring up placing him in a nursing home. Paul started the conversation before I even got the chance. He hardly acted like a seventeen-year-old, mature beyond his years.

"Papi, we've all been talking," Paul said. "We read the letter Dad wrote you."

"And when did you do this?" I asked.

"When you were out walking with Dad," Paul said. "I know I shouldn't have read it since it was addressed to you, but you seemed upset and..."

"No, you shouldn't have read it," I snapped at him. "So what have you all been talking about?"

"We want to take care of Dad," Paul said. "Ariel and Luna are working remotely, and school is remote, too, so..."

"I'm moving back home," Luna interjected. "We'll take turns, working in shifts, and we thought maybe we should look into hospice. He can get hospice at home. Couldn't they help, too?"

At first I was annoyed that the three of them made plans without involving me in the discussion, but because they were willing to make such sacrifices, my annoyance quickly faded, overtaken by pride and love. I sat there and listened to the reasoning behind their decisions.

"Dad said he didn't want you to be his caregiver," Paul said. "He said nothing about us."

"Paul's right," Luna said. "With the help from hospice, we think we can do it. We want to do this. Dad belongs here. He was born here and should die here and not in a nursing home, especially right now. You would die if you couldn't see him, if you couldn't be there for him, with him."

"We can turn the family room into a bedroom and that way he can look into the lake any time he wants," Ariel said. "Then you don't have to worry about him falling down the stairs, and maybe you'd get some sleep. What do you think?"

"We want to do this," Paul reiterated.

"We don't want you to do this alone," Luna said. "You're on the verge of a complete breakdown, and you'll place him in a nursing home just because Dad said you could. I don't think you really want to do that, do you? He has us. You have us, Papi."

"We haven't heard how you feel about it," Ariel said to me.

"Because no one's stopped to ask me," I said.

"We're asking you now," Ariel said.

"I'd like him to stay home," I said.

"So do you agree with the plan?" Luna asked.

"What about your own lives?" I said. "I don't know if your dad would want you to give up your lives for him."

"We owe our lives to you and Dad," Luna said. "You chose to adopt us. We wouldn't have these lives without you."

"You don't owe us anything," I stated.

"There's nothing else to do, anyway," Paul said.

"Yeah, we might as well make ourselves useful," Luna said. "And this is what we want to do. We want you to enjoy your time with Dad... whatever time he has left."

They were all so determined, and I was grateful to have them. Terry and I raised three terrific kids. I took them up on their offer.

As planned, we turned the family room into a bedroom. It worked out great with one exception: Terry didn't want to sleep downstairs because he had never slept downstairs. He was aware enough to know that his bed was upstairs with me. No matter what Paul and Luna did, he found his way back upstairs to me. Of all the bedrooms, he always knew which one was ours.

His ambulation further declined, and there came a time when he couldn't figure out how to walk up the stairs despite his attempts. At the foot of the stairs, we put up a gate with a stop sign across the threshold. These interventions were good deterrents. So he wouldn't get upset, much to everyone's disapproval, I slept in the family room with him and took a nap during the day before working.

Terry refused to use a walker or sit in a wheelchair, so he continued to walk and fall, usually tripping over his feet. With COVID under control in Vermont, Angie opened the camp for Vermont residents only, which was unfortunate because the kids who needed it most couldn't come.

Summer business was better than it ever was. Families weren't flying anywhere for vacations and Vermont's COVID rates were so low the Inn and Cottages remained full all summer.

After the summer crowds dissipated, I took Terry for walks outside by the lake. Every day he grew more and more tired. He slept more than he'd slept for the past five years, usually dozing off in his rocking chair. His body was shutting down. He aspirated on everything he ate and drank, so he coughed all the time. We chose not to treat his recurring pneumonias because they would only recur. Pain killers alleviated his discomfort. I just wanted him to be comfortable and pain-free.

With my arm hooked around his, I walked him along the grounds. October was one of the prettiest months out here in Vermont. In front of the lake, I sat Terry down on one of the picnic benches. Staring into the water, he looked as though he was remembering something. I wondered what it was.

"The leaves are changing. Aren't they pretty?" I said, not like I was expecting a response, but sometimes he surprised me. He blinked one or two times, his eyes fixed on the lake. "I think this is the same picnic bench I first sat on back in 1980. You made these homemade veggie burgers, and I remember thinking it was weird that you cooked hamburgers and hot dogs even though you were a vegetarian. Of all the places to sit, you sat down next to me. That summer was a great summer, wasn't it? That's when it all started. And to think I didn't even want to go. Our lives would have been so different, huh?"

I placed a hand on his knee, joining him in gazing into the lake. For the past couple of weeks, I'd had something on my mind and had to get it off my chest. This afternoon Terry was alert enough to listen.

"Terry, I've been meaning to talk to you about something," I started. "I know you're tired, and you've put up a great fight, but you don't have to fight anymore. I want you to know that it's okay if you want to go. Don't stick around for me, and Paul will understand. They'll all understand. If you're ready, so am I. We're ready if you're ready."

Tilting my head down, I fought back my tears that I so easily shed. Unexpectedly, Terry brought a hand to the back of my head. "It's okay, Terry," I said, placing my hand over his as his hand slowly patted the back of my head. I cherished these affectionate moments. He brought his arm around me, pressing his forehead against mine. "I love you."

"Scott," he whispered.

"Yeah," I replied, on the verge of breaking down in a combination of disbelief and relief. He hadn't said my name in months.

"Scott."

"I love you," I said again, hugging him. "I love you."

He just wanted to sleep. He was tired... so, so tired.

* * *

Over the next month, Terry stopped eating or doing much of anything. Paul and Luna would attempt to feed him, but he'd just close his mouth and refuse to open it. He spent most days asleep, sometimes in bed, sometimes in his rocking chair. We'd all take turns sitting with him, talking to him, and reminiscing as if he could still hear us. The hospice nurse, Heather, convinced us he could hear us and was listening to every word we said. She had a lot of experience with death and dying, so we wanted to believe her. We had to believe her.

In the early morning of Terry's sixty-first birthday, I knew there was something different about him. Sensing my presence, he opened his eyes as I approached his bed. It was like he was waiting for me. He appeared comfortable and not in any kind of distress. Paul had spent a lot of time with him yesterday. I had a feeling he said what Terry needed him to say, something I said a month ago. As I sat down beside him on his bed, he closed his eyes.

"Hi," I said to him, taking his hand in mine. "Well, I'm glad you waited to say goodbye to me because I would have been pissed if you hadn't waited. I'm sorry. I shouldn't have said that. I don't want those to be my last words to you. God, I'm going to miss you."

He opened his eyes again, his fingers twitching ever so slightly as if he was trying to reach for mine. I took his hand and brought it to my lips.

"Happy birthday," I said. He closed his eyes again. "I'm going to really miss you, but you already know that. I've missed you for a long time. Say hi to your parents for me up there. If there's a heaven, that's where they are and that's where you're heading. Terry... you were so good to me... to us. You've made me so happy. So happy... I couldn't have asked for a better partner... a better husband. You were always my better half. I have to believe we'll meet again someday. I know we will."

Resting my head on his chest, I listened to his faint heartbeat, counting the intermittent beats. Every couple of seconds his heart stopped, only to beat again. His breathing was shallow but not labored until I heard a quiet gasp. There were no more heartbeats to count. As much as I prepared myself for this moment, as much as I told myself it would be a blessing, I didn't feel any sense of relief right there and then.

As I lay there with my head against his chest, I draped my arms around him, overcome with absolute and utter despair and an overwhelming sense of loss I'd never experienced before in my life, nor would I ever experience again. A part of me died. As I sobbed, my body trembled against Terry's warm, yet lifeless body.

Paul and Luna must have sensed something because they stood beside his bed. I had no idea how long they had been standing there. For all I knew, Terry waited until they were in the room to finally go. Luna patted my back while Paul sat on the other side of Terry, tears pouring out of him.

Ariel showed up less than a half an hour later. I hadn't moved from the bed, my head still against Terry's chest. My tears had subsided, but I found myself immobile. After these last few moments, I'd never touch his body ever again.

"The funeral home will be here in an hour," Ariel said, his voice shaking. "Papi, did you hear me?"

Slowly, I got up, staring down at Terry. With his eyes closed, he looked like he was in a peaceful slumber. In a daze, I got off the bed and walked over to the window, Terry's favorite spot in the house. The air was completely still, not even a ripple in the lake.

"He looks peaceful, doesn't he?" Luna said.

The entire lake was peaceful, and I hadn't felt more alone.

"Papi?" Ariel said.

"I'm okay," I lied. "Yeah, he looks peaceful. He died peacefully."

This was going to be the last time I'd see Terry in person. Within an hour, the funeral home would arrive. There'd be no open casket or wake because Terry wanted neither. He wanted to be cremated with a memorial service for close family and friends. I kissed his forehead one last time and proceeded to leave the room.

"Papi, where are you going?" Luna asked.

"I just need to take a walk," I said. "I'll be okay. Stay with your dad."

In my pajamas and bare feet, I walked along the lake. In November, there was a chill in the air but no breeze. Memories of those first two weeks in 1980 came flooding back to me, beautiful memories I'd always cherish. For the past thirty years, Terry and I created hundreds of precious memories. I even had fond memories of the times Terry and I blew up at each other because the making up part was always fun, sometimes worth the blow out in itself.

Wandering around the grounds, I found my way inside the restaurant that was currently closed until the start of ski season. I remembered Terry telling me how much he liked the smell of bacon even though he was a vegetarian. And after we had only known each other for a day, he was the only one who remembered my eighteenth birthday. It didn't seem so long ago.

For nostalgia's sake, Terry never replaced the jukebox in the pub. As I stood alone in the empty pub, I vividly remembered watching Terry sit on a stool in the corner, playing his guitar and singing Simon and Garfunkel. Terry Lachance captivated me from the very beginning. Now, in 2020, I flipped through the music selections that had changed over the years; however, the classics remained.

Within seconds, *Dream a Little Dream* played, one of the first songs Terry and I ever danced to, alone, right here in this pub late one night. As the song played, I envisioned Terry and I dancing. I could still feel him in my arms. I could smell his scent. At the bar, I dug out a bottle of tequila and filled two glasses.

"This one's for you," I said to Terry.

Smiling, I brought the shot glass to my lips and downed it in one chug. It was only ten in the morning, but what the hell? Before chugging down the second shot, I imagined him licking the salt off my fingers and palm. What a great night that was, even with one of the worst hangovers of my life. Even back then, after we had only known each other for a few days, he took care of me. I threw up on him and everything, but he didn't seem fazed by it. I poured another two shots, smiling again, in honor of his memory.

"Love never forgets," I said and downed the next two shots. After the song ended, I returned to the jukebox and replayed the song. I stopped it in mid-song, gravitating toward Simon and Garfunkel's *The Boxer*, a song Terry sang until the end. I could still see him sitting there, playing and singing, his eyes on me the whole time because, let's face it, he had a thing for me since the minute he saw me, but I made the first move, something I'd never let him forget.

There were times when I wondered what my life would have been like if I chose a different path... let's say if I stayed in Massachusetts at my dad's firm and married Aimee. No, I chose the right path.

From the minute I loaded my car that night, I knew I made the right decision. Despite the ups and downs that every couple and family have, we had a near perfect life, and I was going to miss it. Even as he rapidly slipped away these past five years, his smile never changed. Even at the end, he never forgot me.

Although Terry Lachance was gone, we'd never forget his love. He'd always live in my heart until the day I died, which I hoped was not for another thirty or forty years. A part of me died when Terry died, but another part of me was very much alive. There's still a lot of life to live. Terry wouldn't have wanted it any other way.

31

Afterword

I first wrote this story in the spring and summer of 2019, but I didn't pick it up again until the late summer of 2020. I wasn't sure if I ever wanted to publish it because Terry and Scott mean more to me than any other couple I've ever created. Maybe because they are so real.

As a geriatric social worker for most of my professional life, this story hits home to me. The second half of the book, in particular, is inspired by real events, including the adoption of Terry and Scott's children.

When I think of Terry in his later years, I remember a sixty-year-old man I worked with as a nursing home social worker. Tall and thin, he wandered around his unit with the sweetest and gentlest demeanor, a personality possibly similar to Terry's. I never knew him in his younger days. His wife was only fifty-eight with two teenaged daughters.

I remember another married couple whose wife had been working as a nurse unit manager in a maternity ward until a few years prior to her diagnosis of lewy bodies dementia. Although they were in their seventies, they had been very active. The husband continued to be active and completely and utterly distraught with the rapid deterioration of his beautiful wife. As we met in my office, his wife hooked her arm around her husband's. Although she couldn't speak, she recognized her husband and looked at him lovingly. It was heart-wrenching. At that time, her husband wished for a bullet to her head. Her husband wasn't a horrible person. He wanted the suffering to end, knowing that's not how his wife would have wanted to live. I didn't know them for long, but it's an experience that stuck with me and probably always will. She passed away in a geriatric psychiatric unit shortly after.

Love Never Forgets is a story of strength and courage. Many times I've read beautiful stories with realistic LGBTQ protagonists, and I find myself rooting for them, hoping for a happy ending; however, a high percentage of these beautifully written stories do not end happily. Not all LGBTQ stories need to end in tragedy, although some may see this story as a tragedy. I don't.

About the Author

Tristen Rowen earned a Masters degree in social work at Boston College and is a lifelong resident of Massachusetts. For the past ten years, Tristen has worked as a geriatric social worker with extensive experience with adults with Alzheimer's disease. Tristen is an avid concert-goer and music lover as evidenced in Tristen's writing. Although Tristen's stories often involve gay romance between two male characters, much of Tristen's subject matter also focuses on mental illness with the goal of reducing the stigma that continues to exist. With ***Loves Never Forgets***, Tristen hopes readers will gain a better understanding of Alzheimer's disease and its impact on spouses and children while also demonstrating the love and strength many families possess.

You can connect with me on:

- https://tristenrowen.com
- https://twitter.com/tristen2500

Also by Tristen Rowen

A Not So Typical Love: Second Edition

Jordan Cameron is not like most nineteen-year-olds. He's never been on a date, he's never left New England, and he's never fallen in love. He lives in his own world, or so that's what it seems to the average person. No one, not even his thirty-one year old brother, Tim, has ever given him the chance to break free.

With a schizophrenic mother in a group home and a career-obsessed absent father, Tim does the best he can raising someone with Jordan's challenging behaviors. Despite Jordan's diagnosis, Tim refuses to label him because 'labels make us less than human.'

Thirty-year-old Jamie Perron has a history of bad relationships. After his girlfriend kicks him out this last time, his friend, Tim, lets him move in for the summer before embarking on a ten month teaching stint in London. Jamie changes everything Jordan has ever known.

Music is the driving force that draws Jordan and Jamie together. With a similar taste in music, Jamie understands Jordan when no one else does. Never did Jamie think he would develop such an intense, romantic relationship with a strange, quiet, and sullen (yet cute) nineteen-year-old boy through the course of one interesting summer.

This is the summer of Jordan's sexual awakening.

On acres of land in the beautiful countryside of Northeastern Massachusetts, Jordan learns to love, Jamie learns how to be loved, and Tim learns how to let go.

This revised **Second Edition** of ***A Not So Typical Love*** contains a brand new ending.

Elie's Aura

Back in the early 1990s, twenty-two-year-old Elvis Marchand was an aspiring hockey star until a career-ending concussion. After losing his hockey scholarship, he flunks out of college, turning to his one true love: Art. That is, until he meets the quiet and shy seventeen year old high school senior, Elie Reznik.

Plagued with paranoia, hallucinations, and delusions, Elvis oftentimes has difficulty distinguishing between what is real and what is not. Patient, understanding, and smitten with the beautiful and stunning Elvis, Elie understands him when no one else does.

Never before does Elvis, a creative genius with peculiar behaviors, believe he'd ever fall in love, especially with a boy. Not only do Elvis and Elie find love in the most unusual of places, Elie becomes one of Elvis's greatest muses of all time, as well as his greatest love.

Elvis and Elie's relationship spans two decades, complicated by fear, distance, and mental illness.

The book, *Elie's Aura,* is just the beginning.

www.ingramcontent.com/pod-product-compliance
Lightning Source LLC
LaVergne TN
LVHW010611100826
845148LV00014B/2923

* 9 7 8 1 7 3 7 1 8 9 6 0 2 *